THE EARTH MADE OF GLASS

Also by Robert Edric in Picador:

IN THE DAYS OF THE AMERICAN MUSEUM
THE BROKEN LANDS

THE EARTH
MADE
OF
GLASS

Robert Edric

PICADOR

A Picador original

The author would like to thank the Society of Authors
for their generosity

A Picador original
First published 1994 by Picador

a division of Pan Macmillan Publishers Limited
Cavaye Place London SW10 9PG
and Basingstoke

Associated companies throughout the world

ISBN 0 330 32977 4

A CIP catalogue record for this book is available from
the British Library

Typeset by CentraCet Limited, Cambridge
Printed by Mackays of Chatham plc, Kent

For my parents
A & E

Since Hell is divided into as many societies as Heaven, therefore also are there as many Hells as there are societies of Heaven; for every society of Heaven is a Heaven on a smaller scale, and every society of Hell is also a Hell on a smaller scale.

Swedenborg
Heaven & Hell

1691

PART I

1

The eyes of the Inquisitor never faltered. He was momentarily alone, his first interview with the man not yet started, but even though unobserved he did not allow himself to relax. His head barely turned; there was no rustle of his collar, no leathery creak of the jacket he wore. He scanned the room in a smooth and level arc, and took in all there was to see, all there was to know about its contents and the man who lived at their centre, the man whose small and comfortless world he had so abruptly entered.

It was a room that had once been grand, built by another, a room designed for entertainment and society, both of which had long been absent from it. This much was immediately evident to him. Even more powerful was the notion that here was a room in which something of great consequence had once taken place, and a room which, in its shadows and echoes, still contained some faint, sour reverberation of that distant event. He had felt this instantly upon entering, and was convinced of it further as he sat and waited for the magistrate to return. The glimmer of old flames still trembled across the ceiling, and ancient dust rode its gentle eddies from one resting place to another.

It was sparsely furnished, and with no ornamentation other than the few bleak portraits which looked down upon him from the wall above the fire. The faces were poorly executed and indistinct in the dim light, and he searched them in vain for anything of the man he was there to see.

He heard footsteps in the passage outside and returned his gaze to the satchel on the table beside him. He occupied himself in the careful removal of his gloves, tugging a measure of slack into each finger before finally drawing free his hand smoothly and rigidly and with satisfaction, as though he were drawing a sword from its sheath. He looked for a moment into his palm and then turned it and looked just as closely at the backs of his fingers. He was not a vain man, but he was proud of his hands, and anyone witnessing this private act would understand this immediately. No one had ever put the question to him directly, but he was convinced that he would live his life more content as a mute or a cripple than as a man deprived of the use of his hands and the simple pleasure of their veneration.

The magistrate entered carrying a tray upon which sat two glasses and a Delftware jug.

'Do you require more light?' he asked, indicating the candles which burned at the far end of the table.

The Inquisitor shook his head. 'We need not concern ourselves yet with any of the written evidence or depositions.'

'Written evidence?'

'Of very little consequence, I'm afraid. But it exists and we cannot ignore it. As yet it is my only reason for being here.'

The magistrate, Samuel Mercer, handed him a glass, the tremors of the liquid at its rim betraying the shaking of his hand. This, too, the Inquisitor could not ignore.

'Please, put yourself at ease. It is merely a land sale, which the Church Commissioners feel ...' He paused, sipped the watery wine. 'To which they feel a certain unwelcome association has become attached.'

'Is that how they choose to see it?'

6

'And which they believe – which *I* believe – warrants closer examination before the sale is agreed.'

'And this is the sole purpose of your visit?'

The Inquisitor saw immediately that any deception or concealment now would only work against him in the days to come. 'That, and the excavation of your angel. Please, magistrate—'

But Samuel Mercer would not be dissuaded: 'And which would you say was of the greatest importance to your Commissioners?' He drained his own glass in a single swallow, then sighed and put it out of his reach, as though the action were a regrettable reflex. He rubbed a hand over his face.

The Inquisitor guessed him to be sixty or sixty-five, twenty years older than himself.

'I personally am intrigued more by the former than the latter.' He spoke in tones as even and ungiving as his gaze, hoping to learn more from the man by creating intriguing spaces into which he might then be drawn.

Samuel Mercer rose from his seat and stood at the window.

The Inquisitor wondered if the slope of the hill upon which the angel was to appear could be seen from there.

The magistrate turned to face him. 'You are an Inquisitor,' he said.

'That is not my title.' Again there was more to be gained by saying little.

'None the less, that is what you are to us. You are *our* Inquisitor.'

'Men who prefer to see goodness and harmony in the world invite it into their own hearts.'

'No one invited you to this place. You came because you were sent.'

7

'I am merely the agent of some greater power.' And a man who understood all too well the imprecise and shifting line between caution and suspicion, the strand of loss and gain, seizure and abandonment, between the high and low tides of contempt and revulsion, and, afterwards, solicitude and pity; long a wanderer on that cold shore, searching the wrack, his character and emotions forged and burnished by the mould of his labours.

A long silence followed. Other footsteps elsewhere in the house came through its stone walls to them, a door opening and closing, coals being raked.

'My housekeeper,' the magistrate said, grateful for this small release of tension.

'I believe I met her yesterday.'

'She told you where I lived.'

'Ah, yes.'

'You asked her. Surely you must have known.'

The Inquisitor smiled. 'It is difficult to know what to say. I am too accustomed to working in the courts and record houses with men my superiors. I did not intend to patronize or insult her. Please convey my apologies.' He fluttered his hand. He too was grateful that they had retreated to the centre ground of common observation and formality.

'Quite the opposite. She was very flattered. Everyone knew of your arrival here, but she was the first to whom you spoke.'

'Excepting the man who drove the cart upon which I came, the landlord of the inn, the boy who carried my bags and parcels, and the woman who brings me my meals.'

The magistrate held up his hand. 'It would be wise not to disabuse her.'

'Then I have formed my first ally.'

A gust of wind blew smoke into the room and both men turned their faces to avoid it.

8

'You are aware, of course, that the two objects of your investigation are as inextricably bound as though they were the sun and moon of a single day.'

'That is what I am here to discover.' The Inquisitor started to reach for his satchel, but thought better of this and left it where it lay.

'And what you must report upon to your masters?'

'You make them sound—'

'And so what has been laid to rest here these past thirty years will be exhumed and brought unhappily back into the light so that others might pass their own ignorant judgements on this place.'

And on everyone who lives here, yourself included? The Inquisitor was intrigued by the magistrate's choice of words, knowing how easily they might have been avoided.

'My business here might be concluded in a week, days even.'

'And so all your bags are empty?'

'Granted.' The Inquisitor breathed deeply. 'You were here, you know what happened. Your own account . . .'

The eyes of both men fell upon the satchel.

'The house burned and the poor unfortunate woman died,' the magistrate said.

'Forgive me,' the Inquisitor said, this being the cushion to his blow, 'but you deceive yourself more than you deceive me. I am not here to pass judgement on you.'

'Then you too have been deceived. We *await* your judgement. There are those of us here who *crave* it. There are those of us who await the blessing of your judgement just as others crave the taste and whisper of the sacrament wherever it might be sought.' Samuel Mercer returned to his seat and gripped its arms in an effort to control his agitation.

The Inquisitor resisted words of consolation, aware that

9

his purpose might be better served by prodding at these raw emotions while they remained exposed.

'It was not my intention to cause you distress,' he said.

'No?'

Both men acknowledged that a balance had been struck, that an understanding, however fragile or imperfect, now existed between them. Each, in his own way, had explored the other, and each had seen more clearly the divergent paths ahead.

When next the Inquisitor looked outside it was growing dark, and he saw in the small panes his own broken reflection, its outline reduced to essentials of mouth and nose and eyes. Unobserved, he mouthed the word Inquisitor to see it whispered back at him, and to be convinced that it was indeed a mirror image he was regarding and not the face of some other pressed to the glass outside. Inquisitor. He had been called the same before, but never before had he taken any satisfaction in the title. Never before had he felt himself so truly defined by it. And never before had he felt so strongly and undeniably the pulse and heartbeat of the power thus conferred upon him.

Samuel Mercer spoke next. 'There is said to be an indelible black stain in Wartburg Castle where Martin Luther flung his inkhorn at the devil.'

'I have heard the story.'

'And visited the place?'

The Inquisitor shook his head.

'Then neither you nor I will ever know for certain if it is true.'

'That he saw the devil?'

'That he threw his horn.'

There was no time for the Inquisitor to consider any further what he was being told.

'Our angel is the domain of Jonas Webster.'

'Your parson.'

10

'It will not wipe clean our stain, I warn you of that, at the beginning.'

'Is that its true purpose?'

'What else?'

'Then why do you believe so fervently that it will fail?'

The magistrate seemed to sag where he sat. 'Because that particular stain is too black and too deep.'

'Battlefields are planted with corn.'

'And still the ploughs turn up their bones. And with every one the prayer and groan of a dying man.'

'You seem very convinced of this.' Again the Inquisitor was puzzled by the magistrate's choice of words.

'I am.'

'I must tell you that I do not share your conviction.'

'Then you are a man waving his pomander in the face of the pestilence.' Samuel Mercer looked pointedly at the bulge in the Inquisitor's sleeve.

The Inquisitor took out his pomander and handed it over for inspection. It was carved of a single piece of ebony, empty, but still impregnated with the scent of the herbs it once held.

'It belonged to my brother, my twin. I carry it so that I might never forget him. And to accept that I too may for ever be but half of what I ought to be.'

Knowing this, Samuel Mercer handled the intricate black globe as though it were a blown egg, letting the slender gold thread of its chain slide over his fingers before handing it back.

'I gain some small comfort in having it with me at all times,' the Inquisitor said, tucking it back into his sleeve.

Watching him, the magistrate wished that he too had an intimacy he could bring himself to share, that this gentle assault upon him might be equally gently repulsed. But he knew he did not, even though his own store of secrets was large.

'Her screams,' he said absently, faltering, and then staring

11

into the fire, as though he sought there some reason or strength to continue.

'The dying woman's?'

'I hear them still. Just as the ploughmen hear those of the slain and the lost and the forgotten.'

'No man is truly forgotten.'

'Or forsaken? I envy you your conviction.'

The time had come for the Inquisitor to leave. He rose and picked up his gloves. He was a tall man, and although the ceiling hung several feet above him, he was accustomed to much larger rooms and he stooped as he approached the doorway.

Outside the dusk had deepened into nightfall.

The two men parted. One watched the other disappear into the darkness, and the other, neither pausing nor turning, felt himself watched until the moment he knew himself to be invisible.

2

He arrived on the day of the autumn equinox. He was a believer in the creation and regulation of balances, and it pleased him that he should arrive on such a day. It struck him as propitious, a portent of success, and he carried this conviction with him as other men might carry a charm.

His journey from the capital lasted six days. He came north, stayed with the Commissioners' agent in those parts, and then turned east, rising out of the Vale on to the higher land of the moors, which stretched, or so others told him, to the precipitous cliffs of the sea.

The man who drove the cart upon which he sat for the last part of his journey frequently rose in his seat and scanned the land ahead, and when he sat down it was always with a grunt of exhalation. He spat on the hindquarters of the single solid horse which pulled them.

They climbed for two hours and then the land levelled off around them into an endless sea of heather and bracken, with here and there the vivid blaze of scattered furze.

'Is there something you seek?'

The carter shook his head.

'You are familiar with the road?'

It stretched ahead of them, a pale and dusty ribbon, offering no alternatives, deceiving them where it rippled, split

13

and joined, and where it rose like smoke and hovered in the dying heat.

This time the driver half turned, still silent, and showed the Inquisitor his closed mouth as though in emphasis. The man had spoken barely twenty words throughout their journey, and most of these as he left the gate of the city where the agent lived, and before he had been told in greater detail of their destination.

'Today is the equinox, the day when both night and day are of equal length.'

'Signifying what?' He spoke as though he were about to become the victim of a hoax.

'Signifying that the sun is crossing the equator, and that henceforth it will be more below it than above it. Until the day of the vernal when that same order is reversed.'

'And this has some bearing on your journey?' This time the man rose, grunted and spat in a single motion. The Inquisitor felt himself mocked.

'My journey has been a long one.'

The carter pulled tight his reins and they stopped.

The Inquisitor wondered if some further objection were being made. He watched the man, heard the horse's laboured breathing.

After a minute his uncertainty turned to anger. 'Are we close by?'

But the carter only shrugged.

'Then I command you to—'

'Over there.'

'What?' The Inquisitor rose and looked to where the man pointed. A line of figures moved through the distant bracken. Dust rose round them, and through it a succession of glints signalled that the figures were brandishing scythes and that they were moving forward in a single body, cutting as they came.

14

'Do you know them?'

'I live in the Vale.'

And here were the natives of a hostile land.

The man flicked the horse back into motion.

They came closer to the line of harvesters, and the Inquisitor saw that they were all women. Each wore a rough scarf which covered her hair and hooded her eyes, with another wound like a visor round her nose and mouth. It was impossible to say who was young and who was old, only to distinguish between those who were tall or short, fat or thin. They moved as one, the same fluid motion of their blades into the vegetation ahead of them.

'Stop,' the Inquisitor said.

The carter was slow to respond.

'Call and ask them how far we have yet to go.' He was still not accustomed to the common manner of speech in the district.

'I know how far we have to go.'

He detected fear in the man's reluctance.

They approached unnoticed until one of the women leaned back with her hands on her hips. She pulled down the lower of her scarves and immediately communicated what she saw to the others. She removed her second scarf and the Inquisitor saw that she was a young woman, barely a woman at all, and that this sudden confrontation frightened her. Another of the women moved to stand between her and the road.

'Good day,' the Inquisitor called to them.

No one answered him.

He heard the carter laughing at him beneath his breath.

Behind the women the bracken lay cut in a swath as straight and as clean as though a single giant blade had been swung through it.

Moving closer still to the harvesters, the Inquisitor saw that many were bare-legged, with their skirts fastened up into

15

their belts, and that they all wore clumsy wooden shoes in the Dutch fashion to protect their feet.

The carter ran a hand through his short black hair.

The Inquisitor withdrew his gaze from the tanned limbs and found himself looking instead at the stains of dried phlegm on the horse's flanks, each now with its circle of flies as though these were wild animals come to water in the heat.

Then the carter made some obscene remark to the nearest of the women, and before the Inquisitor could reprimand him he shook the reins and set them in motion.

'I demand that you apologize.'

'Not to them,' the man said, waiting several seconds before adding, 'And not to you.'

The little that remained of their journey they completed in silence.

3

Jonas Webster prostrated himself between the eyes of his great angel, above him only the cloudless expanse of a drained sky. The risen sun lay beyond the curve of the earth and did not intrude upon his own radiated light. His legs and arms were splayed, and he clutched at the short grass beneath him as though he were in danger of sliding off the slope. He laughed out loud. Insects moved within the cropped sward, and their noises, and that of the grass itself, came magnified to his ears in a chorus of exultation.

'O Lord, O Lord,' he whispered. 'Look down upon Thy servant and know that You have upon this wretched earth the most obedient of men.'

He brushed a fly from his lips.

There was no magnificent angel as yet, only the broad sweep of the hillside through which it would shortly appear. But so great was the vision in Jonas Webster's mind that it seemed to him that the figure already existed. The eyes alone would contain his entire body, the outstretched wings reach to the edge of the curtain of grass; giant hands pressed together in redemptive prayer beneath the globe of his own stomach.

He sat up and looked at the village below. His own home stood prominent, but the rest of the cottages and cruder dwellings lay hidden amid rutted lanes and small orchards. Only the house of the retired magistrate challenged his own in

17

standing. Beyond, all was lost in the wash of haze not yet risen. Thin pillars of smoke rose unwavering in the still air.

'See them toil, Lord,' he said. 'They are your beasts of the field. And I too shall toil in the revelation of Your glory. Believe me. And give me the strength and the conviction to see my work here to its conclusion. Give me these just as You sent me my vision. Let this place be blessed and cleansed now and for all time to come, and let men turn to You upon this hillside, and in doing so turn their backs upon the wickedness and the misery of this world.'

He was pleased with himself. This hillside was his altar; soon it would become his cathedral. At the foot of the Lord's angel, where his feet protruded from his gown, would be carved the initials JW and the year of its creation. He too was a man who believed in the potency and grace of providential dates.

He was distracted by a cry, and looking between his legs he saw his wife at the foot of the slope. She was calling to him and waving vigorously, a cloth in each hand like a signaller upon a ship. She was an ant amid ants.

'Silence, woman,' he said aloud.

Her cries continued. Around her, some common motion in the labour of the other ants showed that they too had been alerted by her.

'Forgive her, Lord.'

She started to climb towards him.

A tree was felled in a distant copse and the noise of its drop and the crash of its boughs and branches disturbed the wider silence. The charcoal burners had arrived. It was their season in the woodlands of the estate. They were men made black by their work and they lived with their work and then went as they had come, silent, unannounced and unwelcome. People stayed out of the trees for the duration of their visits, and only afterwards went to inspect the blackened craters of their cold stacks and to salvage for themselves what might remain after the land agent had been with his carts. They were devils, not men, idiots and outcasts who deliberately sought the anonymity of their trade.

Two had once tried to gain entry into Jonas Webster's church and he had driven them from it with a staff. And only when he had exhausted himself with his beating, spurred on by the cries of his congregation, did he discover that one of these black forms was a woman. Her jacket was torn and her breast revealed. The other had helped her to her feet and they had fled together. 'Thank me, thank me,' Jonas Webster had called after them.

They came in the early autumn with the first inch of leaves and would play darkness to his blinding light until ten days beyond All-Hallows. And for that time the world was not safe. Another precarious balance was struck and men were careful to maintain it. Elsewhere, they stole children; elsewhere, they lay with their mothers and daughters and beasts of the yard.

Another call, another distraction from these thoughts grown sermon awaiting only its garland of scripture.

His wife was resting. She did not know where the folds of the garment would hang, where the legs would become body, the stomach chest. She did not know where the graceful neck would rise from the scrape of collar bone, or where the tips of praying fingers would incline towards a heart.

She wanted him to go down to her. She wanted him to stand beside her, to put his arms around her and let the light which fell upon him fall upon her.

Another sound caught his ear. This time from the hillside above him. The ground was struck, and struck again, and the vibrations trembled into his palms.

Two men came over the rim of the upper earth and beat upon the ground with staves.

19

He watched them as they came and saw them stop the instant they saw him. Both were in his employ, and both had been allowed to share in his vision of the angel. But to them this vision was a thickness of turf to be cut, a depth of soil to be dug clear. To them it was the problem of drawing a straight line over curved land, and of ensuring that what was viewed close to upon the hillside appeared in correct proportion when viewed from below. They were not educated men, neither devoted to their work nor inspired by it. Their labour elsewhere was unreliable.

Jonas Webster rose to meet them.

Fifty years earlier both had fought at Marston Moor, one on the side of the Parliamentarians, and the other carrying a pike in the service of the King. The first had lost the lower part of his right leg, and the other two fingers and a piece of his jaw. They had been boys then and had come home to cauterize their wounds and minds, and to repeat their story ever since. When the man with the injured jaw spoke it was as though he did so with his tongue pushed hard into his cheek, and what he said was largely unintelligible, except to the other, who acted as his interpreter.

'You are engaged upon my work?' Jonas Webster asked them.

'And the Lord's.'

'Of course. Testing the ground to see where we might best proceed?'

'Pits have been dug and the chalk taken out.'

'Surely not. By whom?'

Both men shrugged. The one with the injured leg lifted his stump and tapped the ground.

'He feels the depth of soil better than I can with my stave,' the other said, and laughed.

'But who would have excavated these pits? I see no pits.'

20

'Filled in. Men who lived in caves, the magistrate reckons. Men who lived on the moors when all manner of beasts walked up there alongside the Jews turned to wolves.'

'That's a nonsense and you'll not repeat it in my company,' Jonas Webster said. He meant the beasts, not the Jews; some falsehoods he was happy to feed; some falsehoods contained their grain of truth turned precious pearl.

'The pits are still dug.'

'Sir.'

'Sir.'

The word pricked Jonas Webster. 'Then we must plot where these depressions lie and make our calculations around them.'

'Calculations around them.'

'Plot them on your drawing, you mean?' The man pulled from his jacket the crude outline Jonas Webster had given them. It contained only a sketch – an angel as an angel might be drawn by any man, visionary or sceptic. A dry watercourse was marked in arrows along one thigh. Another, winter-bourne, rose in its gulley at the angel's shoulder. An outcrop of rock pierced the feathers of a wing.

'All needs to be took into account,' the man said.

Jonas Webster snatched the drawing from him. He refused to have his vision spoiled before it lay revealed. Its whiteness would blind his detractors. They would shrink to insignificance before it. They would grow ugly and deformed in the light of its beauty and perfection. They would sicken, die, and be buried in full sight of its everlasting vigour.

He silently cursed these men who could not see and understand what he could see and understand. He cursed their blindness and ugliness and deformity.

'Your wife,' the man with the missing jaw said.

The woman was now little more than a hundred feet

21

beneath them. She rested, panting and breathless on the angel's arm.

'Go and give her assistance.'

Neither man moved for a moment and then both half walked, half slid down the slope to where the woman awaited them. Jonas Webster watched her hold out her arms to them. And he cursed her too for having brought her feeble complaints and domestic concerns on to his altar.

'Jonas,' she said as she approached him, pulling free of the two men and wiping her hands where they had held her.

He looked down at her and saw only the smoke which rose from her and the sheen of sweat which covered her face. The men stood small beneath her and turned their backs on him.

She came closer. Tearful in her exertions, she collapsed at his feet. He looked up and held out both his arms – as he had once thought his angel might hold out his own. He looked down at her, but could not bring himself to kneel and comfort her. He hoarded his blessings as other men hoarded gold, and gave them out in the same manner as these others paid their creditors.

He told her to rise and stop making a spectacle of them both. He had spent a sleepless night in expectation of the news she brought.

4

'You might say that I was a storm-beaten vessel happy to find safe harbour.' The magistrate cleared the table of old papers.

'But still a young man, surely?'

'Young, yes, but worn down by my trials. The prospect then of living to an age such as I have reached under a similar burden . . .'

'And so you for ever afterwards hugged the shore.'

'"And ventured not out on to waters broad and deep." Do you read poetry?'

'Little time.'

In the few days they had been acquainted the two men had grown to appreciate the company of the other. There was little social intercourse in the place above the common mix of families, neighbours, and labourers.

But the Inquisitor was still an Inquisitor, and the magistrate still the focus of his inquisition. Neither man could forget this, and their tangential courtesies and other unspoken signals betrayed the fact every time they met. The Inquisitor had written in his journal that there was a deviousness in their conversations which he truly regretted. He also noted that on each occasion he called to see Samuel Mercer, the man made a point of stopping the clock which ticked loudly and woodenly on the chest beside them. He said this was done so they might talk undisturbed by its ticking and chiming, but the Inquisitor could not entirely dismiss from his mind the idea that it was done in some way to deny their time together. He had not broached the subject. If it was a denial, then it was one easily achieved, and if the other man derived some illusory comfort from it, then he in turn would not deny him this. It remained another of their unspoken agreements.

'You were working,' he said.

'Old cases. I do little. My father and grandfather were magistrates before me, my father-in-law a judge. Useless momentum.'

'Here in the North?'

'Latterly.' The magistrate closed a heavy volume with a louder slap than was necessary. 'Fortunes made in suffering and lost early in some misguided Indies speculation.'

It occurred to the Inquisitor that something of the man's buried sadness or regret was about to be revealed to him, but then saw by the way Samuel Mercer left the table and busied himself among the shelves of his books that he had drawn back, that he did not yet possess the strength or the conviction to strike that hard or that deep into himself.

He is fearful of what he might reveal, thought the Inquisitor.

'The plague was here, did you know that?' Samuel Mercer returned to the table with a ledger so ancient that its dried calf binding resembled nothing more than a bed of desiccated mud at the bottom of a long empty lake. Pieces fell from it as he turned the cover. Any secrets the volume contained were about to be exposed to the light of day for the first time in decades.

'Not recently? Not the London plague?'

'No. Though there were many came this far in fleeing from it.'

'Did anyone come here, to this place?'

'No.' The answer was given too forcibly. A yellow page

slid free of its binding. 'Not to settle here. Why should they? Not from London.'

It was not what the Inquisitor had asked. 'But people passed through here on their journeys elsewhere.'

'Elsewhere,' the magistrate echoed.

'I believe there was a hermitage and refuge on the moors.'

'It still exists. Monks. Much further to the east, within sight of the sea.' Samuel Mercer ran his fingers over the loose pages, only then aware of their dislocation.

'And no one here suffered?'

'No one.'

Except the woman who died. Say it.

'I was speaking of the Great Plague. "The Death" as it was called.'

'But that was over three hundred years ago!'

'Three hundred and fifty. These things persist. They are pedestals to our history.'

Such a clumsy phrase, thought the Inquisitor.

'Do you wish me to tell you that the pestilence in the capital and the death of the woman were somehow connected?'

There was a small pressure to be maintained. 'You might tell me it was only coincidence.' The Inquisitor waited.

'I won't lie to you.'

'I knew that the moment I met you.' *Ogni vero non e buono a dire*, thought the Inquisitor. By virtue of suppression do we lie.

The magistrate seemed surprised. 'Thank you. You are, of course, aware by now that she was killed as a witch.'

'Hysteria. Wild imaginings.'

'They say an entire family in a neighbouring place was killed during the Death because it was believed they had encouraged its arrival there by being dismissive of its potency.'

As dismissive as I was about the cause of the woman's

25

death? 'You were going to tell me about the plague.' On this occasion the Inquisitor was content to draw back from the thirty-year-dead woman. He was content to walk in ever-decreasing circles around the facts of the matter; content to clear his way steadily amid the thickets of hearsay and specu-lation, to cut a path through the tangle of wilful conjecture and prejudice. He was a woodsman coppicing an old wood. Sturdy growths were his truths, the strangle of undergrowth his deceits.

'The village died,' the magistrate said. 'All is recorded here. Of a hundred and thirty souls, ninety-three succumbed. Forty children. The Lord visited this place with severe and malign intent.'

'And those who did not suffer?'

'Who were they? The men who lived having lost their wives and children? The children who survived as friendless orphans?'

It surprised the Inquisitor to hear him talk with such passion, as though this catastrophe had been recent, and as though he himself had suffered in it.

'Many fled up on to the moors.'

'And lived there?'

'And died there. There was some belief that the higher land and fresher air would keep them free of the vapours upon which the destruction was carried. But it was not to be. They died where they struggled to survive, and many who were buried lie in unmarked graves.'

'Is that why people here are reluctant to leave the marked paths?'

'Our women are more formidable than our men. Their work takes them up there more often. We are all superstitious creatures.'

'Have any remains ever been unearthed?'

26

'Why do you ask?'

'I was merely curious as to procedure.'

'You mean would they be brought back here for a decent Christian burial?'

It was not what the Inquisitor had meant. 'Yes.'

'Very unlikely. For, in the words of our parson, how would we know which were the bones of Christian men and which the bones of men too stupid or ignorant to have taken God into their hearts? There is also some confusion as to which are the bones of men and which the bones of animals. You see our – his – dilemma.'

'But the village survived?'

'Not on this site. Half a mile to the north. Greatly overgrown; nothing to see now but marks upon the ground.'

The magistrate searched through the loose papers. 'Some of the records are illegible. Our parson at the time was one of the first to succumb. It is said that he died a month before any of the others, that his suffering was prolonged and great, and that after ten days of lonely agony when his body boiled and burst he finally denounced his master. It is said that after those ten terrible days he somehow found the strength to rise from his sick-bed, wrap his soiled blanket around his naked body and crawl into the church, there to make his awful denunciation. He died upon the altar and there he rotted, his diseased breath and the odour of his decay fouling the place for ever.'

'Then it is not the present church?'

The magistrate shook his head. 'If the Lord could visit his own servant in such a terrible manner, then what did he intend for the remainder of his flock? What, indeed, did he intend for the sinners? Be sure, then as now, they knew who they were.'

'The past forever sheds its light on the present.' Before the words had left his lips, the Inquisitor regretted uttering them.

27

'Precisely,' said the magistrate. 'And mysterious are the dispensations of Providence.'

For the first time the Inquisitor saw above the hearth the panel of framed embroidery in which the names of the magistrate and his dead wife were stitched, and with the names of four children, three girls and a boy, sewn around the borders. It was beyond him to ask to look at it any more closely.

'You came here to take up some offered position?'

'To grow old. Forgive my flippancy. Yes, I came here so that my wife' – did he turn, did he half turn, did his eyes flick towards the chimney breast? – 'might be closer to her family. She was an only daughter, an only child, at a time when such things were precious. Her father presided over the Northern Circuit. I don't deny that he was helpful in my own career, such as it was. It may interest you to know – and this time I will allow the coincidence – that he and Hopkins were acquainted, and that the two men shared each other's company when their paths crossed.'

'Then the coincidence is doubled because I myself met the man as a child.'

'I, too.' It was a regrettable admission, hair's breadth from confession.

The Inquisitor took the ledger and scanned several of its pages without interest.

'My wife died in childbirth,' the magistrate said unexpectedly. 'Elizabeth.' He spoke the name with fondness, silently repeating it as though it were a sweet taste in his mouth.

'My condolences.'

'That too was a long time ago. It was always her mother's wish that we should live close by them, but I could not live in the judge's pocket. I could not think then that this earth contained a place for sufferings and terrors so unmanning.'

The Inquisitor waited in silence for the waves of this

anguish to subside. He had visited the small churchyard, but had searched only for the grave of the woman. It was his turn now to divert them from their sorrowful course.

'And was the new village rebuilt by the survivors of the pestilence?'

'I cannot say. Some must have come back down from their refuge. Most, it is said, made their way to the coast. There is an abbey there, on the cliff.'

'I have heard of it.'

'There is a point on the road eight or nine miles from here where you might mount a standing stone and on a clear day see it.'

'Is it a prosperous place?'

'The port beneath dispatches ships and men into the Northern waters in pursuit of the whalefish.'

'That, too, I have heard.'

'You speak as though all you truly believe is the evidence of your own eyes.'

'Then I shall consider myself rebuked.'

The two men laughed.

'An unreformed sceptic,' the Inquisitor confessed. 'The nature of my work.' Qualities and failings bestowed upon me by other men.

'There was a man who lived here who sailed into the ice, and who returned after an absence of three years to tell us a tale of seeing ice bears in such great profusion that they reminded him of nothing more than a flock of sheep grazing peacefully in a meadow.'

'And was he believed?'

'Oh, greatly. Who were we to dispute him? And the more he repeated the story, so the larger grew the flock. Likewise the size and the ferocity of the fishes he speared.'

'What became of him? Is he sailing still?'

'He returned to the hunt the following year and he and his shipmates and their vessel disappeared.'

The time had come for parting, and as the Inquisitor rose to leave he passed close by the embroidered names and committed them all to memory.

5

The next day he walked on the moor. The women worked again amid the bracken, cutting it for bedding for their stock in the absence of straw, and making fires of its fibrous roots and stems.

He approached close to them. They had seen him at a distance and were this time not alarmed by his appearance.

He greeted them and they stopped their work. It was known why he was there, but some knew one thing and others another.

'Good morning. Please, don't let me stop you.'

'We were ready to stop.'

The Inquisitor recognized Samuel Mercer's housekeeper.

The women gathered around him, sat on the ground, and removed their scarves.

'You come up Jacob's Ladder?' one of them asked him. She was the girl to whom he had spoken upon his arrival. One of the others slapped her shoulder and told her to hold her tongue. The girl refused. 'Parson Webster's steps. We call it Jacob's Ladder.'

'Angels ascending and descending between Heaven and earth,' he said, raising and lowering his hand.

'He read it to us.'

The path had consisted of crude steps hewn into the rock.

'He had it cut so as to come and go and oversee his work

there,' another told him. Most were now keen to be included in the conversation.

'He told us we were not to use it, but we do.'

He spoke with them at length about the angel, and their remarks concerning it were largely dismissive. This surprised him. They would believe in the figure only when they saw it. The younger women and girls were the most eager to talk.

'We heard tell of that chalk giant,' one of them said, her hand over her mouth.

'They said him like a bull.'

The older women continued to slap them for what they said, but the gentle blows were all part of the fun and dare in telling, and the Inquisitor understood immediately his role as a novelty in the proceedings.

'I have seen only horses,' he said. 'Sites of pagan worship, I believe.'

'And they let them stand?' the housekeeper asked him.

'I believe so.'

'And ours is to be the first angel?'

'Better were the place left alone.' This came from the oldest of the women. She sat to the rear of the group and ate an onion. She dabbed with a cloth at the cuts on her legs. The others too bled from countless small abrasions.

'Do you have no water?' the Inquisitor asked them. He was concerned for their injuries, but aware too of how the old woman might interpret his concern.

'Not up here,' the girl answered him.

'But I'm certain I passed a small pond on my arrival.' He estimated where he had seen this from his vantage point on the cart, and pointed. He was surprised to see that none of the women followed his arm.

'We know about that place.'

'Oh?'

'Look atop it.' It was the old woman again. She pointed up, above where the Inquisitor had indicated. A sheet of low, thin cloud covered the sky, but where she pointed a patch of blue shone through.

'The sun to warm your backs,' he said.

This time even the youngest lowered their faces.

'What is it? Does it have some significance?'

'It is where the Devil himself fell from heaven to earth.'

He should have guessed. Countless other fractures and clefts had been pointed out to him in the past.

'And the pond was where he struck?'

'And went on through the earth straight to his fiery kingdom,' the girl said, nodding vigorously.

'And that is why you cannot drink from the water collected there.'

They nodded in unison.

'For fear of what?'

'For fear of him rising like a serpent and seizing anyone foolish enough to stop to admire their reflection as they drink.'

'Have many been lost?' He kept all mockery out of his voice.

'In times past. Travellers, mostly. Come on to the moors and not knowing.'

'But no one from the village?'

'Who would be so foolish, knowing what we know?'

'Of course.'

The challenge had been small and he had not risen to it.

'I have looked into it,' the old woman said, her eyes fixed on the Inquisitor. Her remark surprised the others more than him and they responded with a round of disbelieving nos and nevers and whens.

'Fifty years ago,' she said.

The Inquisitor knew this before she spoke.

'It's why you are here,' she said to him. She returned to wiping the blood from her feet and shins. There was confusion among the others. Several of the older ones put down their own food and watched her.

She'll say no more, the Inquisitor thought. She merely wanted to let me know.

'And was it black as night and still as a looking-glass?' the youngest asked daringly.

The old woman's eyes never left those of the Inquisitor. 'It was.'

'And did it teem beneath its surface with all nature of creatures?'

'Don't answer her, don't say,' another shouted, covering her ears.

'It did,' the old woman said to the Inquisitor.

'Then you were fortunate indeed,' he said.

'Fortunate?'

'Not to be seized and dragged down.'

'No, no, no.' The woman who had covered her ears rose and ran into the bracken with her hands still pressed to her head. Several others rose alongside her, but ran only a few paces before returning.

'I was indeed fortunate,' the old woman said.

The Inquisitor saw that she took no real pleasure in telling him this.

'It was a terrible time,' he said, hoping to suggest in the minds of the younger ones that he was talking of the war unknown to them.

'A man might drown in a bowl of water if it is God's will,' said one who had not before spoken.

'Amen.'

The Inquisitor regretted this turn in their conversation. It was as though the cloud above them had suddenly fallen, darkening as it came.

'We know not to cut there.'

'Know to leave it well alone.'

'We planted around with parsley so that—'

'Fool's parsley.'

'So that he might hear our curses carried down to him on its roots.'

The old woman rose and walked away from them.

When she was out of earshot, the girl asked the Inquisitor what she had meant about his reason for being there.

'I don't know.'

'It was the woman who burned,' another told her.

'What has that to do with the pool?'

'How many of you were living here at the time?' the Inquisitor asked them.

Only the ones who had not been born called out their names. Four others turned their backs on him and picked up their scythes.

They all returned to their work until only the girl remained beside him.

'My father is the stonemason,' she told him. 'Mother died. I don't need to do this, only there is nothing else this time of year.'

He saw the blood dried in thin brown lines along her arms and legs.

'Is it true that the devil once lived in Heaven and was cast out?'

'True or not, it is what many people believe.'

'Do *you* believe it?'

The Inquisitor sighed. 'Yes, I believe it.'

'Then I shall believe it. Except why would God wish to punish us in that way?'

'I don't know.'

'I sometimes wonder—' She stopped and looked to where the others had resumed their work.

'About God?'

'No, about the earth. I sometimes wonder how it would be if in some places under all the bracken and grass and soil the earth was to be made of glass so that we might see straight through it and into Hell below.' She became nervous – whether at the nature of her suggestion or her temerity in making it, he could not tell.

'To know for certain that it existed?'

'Oh, I know that it exists,' she said. 'In my heart I know it exists.'

'Then why?'

'So that we might just *see* it. So that we might just *see* it and *know*.'

She left him and her words stayed with him for the rest of the day.

He walked to where he believed he had seen the pond, but was unable to find it. He sought to orientate himself by the guiding finger of sunlit sky, but that too had withdrawn and all above him the cloud was sealed tight.

6

Two days later he crossed the moor alone to visit the standing stone from which he might see the edge of the world and the ruin of the abbey, beneath which lay the port from which the man of the village had sailed to his death in the ice. It was no part of his work there, but that work was no longer the simple task he had anticipated, and might be equally well served by discursive as well as direct enquiry. Six months earlier he had made application to the Commissioners for some promotion; this investigation, he now believed, was his test.

He left at dawn, before the sun had seeped down upon the village like molten metal across a foundry floor, and before there was anyone about to ask him where he was going, and why. He left by the path which skirted the churchyard and climbed the hill alongside the road.

Below, only Jonas Webster watched him go, angry at the audacity of the man in crossing his precious slope when all others had been warned off. He stood in the church doorway and watched until the Inquisitor was silhouetted against the brightening sky at the crest of the rise. His damnations were a swarm of fleas settled over them all.

The Inquisitor was blinded by the sun. He came up into it and the strongest of its early rays embraced him. He stood in it with his eyes tight shut. It was still cold, the night having not yet fully withdrawn, but already there were countless small mists rising and feathering and burning away where the moisture from the land was driven off. It was something he had never before seen on such a scale and he stood beguiled by it.

He walked quickly, determined to cover the ground away from the village before anyone followed him in pursuit of their own labours.

He walked for two hours with the same even stride. And then he stopped. The land fell gently away from him in every direction, all boundaries lost in the haze of heat and distance. Here and there a narrow path or trod intersected his own, and on occasion his own road forked, forcing him to follow the line which seemed to him to continue most directly along the one he had already come. He rose upon every slight prominence to search for the standing stone.

He saw it an hour later, more distant than he had expected. His shadow was reduced to its smallest pool and he calculated that it was noon. So distant was the stone that it had been more of an encouragement when out of sight. But his path to it was now downhill and he soon reached it.

It rose twice his own height and he saw immediately that he would be unable to surmount it as the magistrate had suggested. He wrapped his arms around it and estimated its circumference. It tapered slightly towards its top, and he saw by the irregularity of this that the stone was incomplete. It stood in a small hollow into which the surrounding heather did not intrude.

He searched towards the sea and was disappointed with what he saw. He was alone in the world, had become its centre and pivot.

He ate the food he carried with him.

He searched the crude monument for any indication as to the men who had erected it, but found only what might or might not have been the tip of a crescent moon, and a line of weathered stone rounded at one end and pointed at the other which might or might not have been the hind leg of some creature. He was angry with himself for having expected so much more.

His road back grew hard and dusty, and whenever the opportunity arose he left it and followed the runs of green turf which here and there cut through the denser vegetation.

He came upon the remains of no strange creatures, nor the bones of men who had perished fleeing the lower ground.

On several occasions the side paths he followed came to dead ends and he was forced to turn back and seek out another way. Wherever he went he made sure he could see the long pale stripe of the road. Only once did he lose sight of this, and the instant he realized what had happened he retraced his steps to where he had last seen it, and afterwards followed it more closely to its western rim.

It was early evening by the time he reached the edge of the moor. The ground dropped beneath him and he took several strides with his eyes closed so that he might then open them and surprise himself with the distant view over the Vale ahead as it was more and more revealed to him.

It was as he walked in blindness that the voice of Jonas Webster came to him.

'Did you hope to visit some other place?'

He opened his eyes and for an instant was just as blinded by the setting sun as he had been by it newly risen. He looked around him, blinking away dead stars.

'I walked to your standing stone.'

Still he could not see the man.

'Not *our* standing stone. Merely the blasphemous symbol of some Godless others.'

'Whatever you say.'

The man had been sitting or crouching close by, and he

now rose as though intent upon making a trick of his sudden appearance.

He was the same age as Samuel Mercer, perhaps a little younger, and though the Inquisitor had anticipated that the two men might have had a great deal in common, he had been quickly disabused of this. He disliked the man's sanctimony, the unshifting block of unassailable piety upon which he rose every time he spoke. Physically, too, Jonas Webster repulsed him. His eyes were divergent, and protruded – not to any great degree, but to the extent that no man standing directly before him could be certain which eye regarded him, and to a degree which gave him the appearance of constantly being in a state of slight but unsettling puzzlement or alarm.

It had been suggested to the Inquisitor that upon his arrival he might seek lodgings with the man, but after meeting him this was unthinkable.

'It is my intention to erect a fence across the top of the slope,' Jonas Webster said, indicating the hill.

The Inquisitor knew then that he had been watched ascending.

The man came towards him with his hands tucked into his cuffs like a monk.

'A marvellous view.'

Jonas Webster did not turn to examine it. 'You think so? There is nothing there. The most magnificent view of all is the view into our own hearts to see the wonders that reside there.'

'The Lord created all this too.'

But Jonas Webster would not be drawn.

'You smashed off the top of the stone in your efforts to topple it,' the Inquisitor said, the realization barely formed as his words gave it substance.

The parson looked at him hard, his two lips acceptance and denial.

'It is deeply rooted,' he said eventually.

'But nevertheless you managed to chisel it clean of its carvings and inscription.'

'What inscription? There were no words upon it. It was an abomination, pointing Heavenwards in bestial mockery.'

Then it *had* been the hind leg of a creature. Or perhaps the thigh and calf of a man with the creature obliterated at his front.

'You turn truths and comforts into lies and suspicions, sir.' He surprised himself at the bluntness of his criticism.

Jonas Webster grimaced at this, but said nothing.

A bird rose suddenly out of the ground at the Inquisitor's feet and he stepped backwards, startled, and Jonas Webster laughed aloud, as though this too were another of his tricks.

7

He visited the stonemason's yard on the edge of the village and there he encountered the other angels created in that place. It amused him to see them, so many winged and penitent bystanders, praying for strength and deliverance surrounded by the blocks and chippings and dust out of which they had risen, and amid which they awaited their own impossible recall to Heaven. Some were dwarves, dressed for the graves of the young and the newborn dead, and some were cut in human form to cast their warming shadows over the fully grown.

One stood four feet higher than the Inquisitor, and he stopped before this figure, looked up into its empty eyes and spoke to it. It looked impassively down at him, as though in worldly consideration rather than celebration of the corpse above which it was intended to stand sentinel.

'You look down on us all,' the Inquisitor said.

'And likes not, I dare say, too much of what he sees.'

The stonemason possessed the neck and shoulders of an ox. He wore an apron, beneath which he was naked to the waist, and so completely was he covered in the fine dust of his labours that, motionless, he looked like one of his own recent creations. He wiped his mouth, cleared his nose, and licked clean his lips.

'I was admiring your angel.'

'You do recognize him, then?'

'The Archangel,' the Inquisitor said.

42

'Commissioned but never paid for. It was once a service of mine but little in demand these days.'

'I would be proud to have him stand above my own grave.'

'In glorification of yourself or the power above?'

The Inquisitor knew who had made this criticism of the man.

'Will he speak to me?'

'I dare say.'

The two men walked together round the yard.

The Inquisitor had visited other homes in the village – tenant farmers, the miller's agent, a water bailiff who lived there but worked five miles away where the stream which ran alongside the village road broadened sufficiently for its fishes to grow and its osier banks to be cultivated – but nowhere else had he encountered anyone so at ease in his presence (he would not call it company) as the stonemason. The questions he asked of these others solicited the same cautious answers, and he learned little he did not already know.

The man showed him the work upon which he was presently engaged – dressing stone for the house of the landowner who employed the bailiff.

'Simple work that I might easily enough employ an apprentice at were there anyone willing to do it.'

'Is there no one?'

'One boy came, but my angels put a fear into him and he stayed away. He said they were not angels at all, but living people turned to stone to which I had added wings.'

'And are they?'

'Some.'

The Inquisitor said that he was surprised that so few of the houses in the village were built of stone, particularly with material of such good quality available so close.

'They cannot bear the cost,' the mason said, his words a

sigh of resignation that anticipated neither argument nor denial. 'You see the yellow in it. Magnesium.'

'The land is poor?'

'Starved enough to fulfil our needs and little more. Most winters we are half under water.'

Close by to the west, on his journey from the agent in the city, the Inquisitor had passed through farmland hedged and dyked and so filled with healthy crops of corn, grass and vegetables that he had seldom seen the like on his travels elsewhere.

'Can the soil not be improved, drained?' he asked, pleased that their conversation was as straightforward as that between any two men passing the time of day, and not shaped and beset by the anxieties and suspicions he encountered elsewhere. In truth, he cared little for the quality of the land or the poverty of the villagers, but was content to show concern for the sake of the conversation alone.

'Did you take any stone from the ruined house?' he asked.

'From the moment you arrived I have been waiting for that question.'

'It is not a judgement upon you.'

'Upon a grave robber, you mean. No, I took none of the stone. To what purpose?'

'Why do you call it a grave?'

The stonemason took out a cloth and wiped his brow and cheeks. Sweat had scored channels through the dust which coated him, marking him like a heathen.

'Perhaps I should say monument. To the terrible work that went on there. Call it what you will, it is of little consequence now.'

'I cannot agree with you,' the Inquisitor said.

Then the mason said a surprising thing: 'Does parson Webster still call her a witch?'

44

It was a simple enough question, but one which suddenly revealed a great deal to the Inquisitor.

'He does,' he said.

'Then I suppose we must believe him and go along with him.'

'And what you believe in your own heart, does that count for nothing?'

'I said we must believe him. And live our lives as best we see fit.'

Although their faces were only inches apart, it was as though the mason had turned his back on the Inquisitor, and he immediately regretted having taken advantage of the man's willingness to speak to him. He had forced him into saying too much and now they were moving apart. It was as though Jonas Webster had come to stand beside them and listen to what was being said.

'If it were within my power to take one of your angels with me when I leave then I would.'

'I doubt any of them will ever leave this place.'

They had arrived in their slow circuit at the stone face of an attractive young woman, beside whom stood three winged girls, decreasing in size and age from her side. The hands of the woman were held not in prayer but spread wide in preparation for embrace.

Before the Inquisitor could comment on this group, the mason's daughter entered the yard and called to her father. She approached, but stopped and turned away from them when she saw where they stood.

'She is daughter, wife and mother to me,' the mason said. 'And soon she will marry and go.'

The Inquisitor was about to make light of this, but remained silent when he saw the depth and the darkness of the sorrow in the man's eyes.

8

The chalk angel took flight in its barest outline during the first full night of the waning moon.

In the morning the first man to go about his business left his home at six, and that man, a tenant farmer in search of a sow that had come untethered and wandered away, looked in the direction of the moor to estimate the time until sunrise, and there in the growing light saw the first white lines etched upon the sward. He forgot his task and ran back to his sleeping wife, to his brother and sister and four children. He woke them and hurried them out to stand alongside him and gaze up at what he had seen. There was pride in his voice, and urgency, and the expectation of some acclaim. He pointed out the lines of the emergent figure to each of them in turn. Those who knew what they were gazing upon stood in the cold morning air and looked in silent awe; and those who cared little for the project fretted to return to their beds. Then, as though this silent celebration of his own family were not enough, the man ran to his neighbours and woke these, and they too came out into the street half dressed and complaining at being woken, fearful of some approaching calamity. And they too saw the angel.

'The edge of his wings,' said one.

'His arms,' said another.

There were four long lines on the hillside, running from the top of the slope to midway down its sweep. It was as though

46

four springs had appeared and the water issuing from each had come down the hillside by the easiest means, scouring away the thin soil and turf until their flow had suddenly ceased and they had sunk back into the ground along the same contour.

'They are not his wings and neither are they his arms,' said the man who had made the discovery. 'The outer lines are the lines of his chest and the inner ones the folds of his robes.'

He in turn was contradicted, and an argument broke out. But his was the discovery, and his interpretation was allowed to stand.

By the time Jonas Webster arrived there were two dozen people gathered, standing singly and in small groups, all with their eyes fixed upon his creation. He passed among them and greeted them. He dispatched boys to rouse and bring out those who were not already assembled.

The speculation and arguments annoyed him and he shouted for silence.

Those woken by the boys came out with reluctance. Some had already heard the commotion, had looked out of their windows to establish its cause, and then returned to their beds. Some were in little awe of the lines, and some were in contempt of them. It had been two years since the parson had claimed the land in readiness for his creation, two years since their few sheep had been able to wander freely upon it.

'I shall say a prayer,' Jonas Webster announced, falling to his knees in a gesture so emphatic that several others around him felt their own knees bend in instant compliance and they too found themselves on the ground with their hands together.

'It is to glory in the magnificence and the charity and the splendour of the Lord above that we find ourselves here.'

Murmured amens.

He went on. Virtues were extolled and a multiplicity of blessings counted. The angel was as nothing compared to the

47

gifts of the Lord, the merest gesture of gratitude in return for the spiritual wealth flung down in golden showers upon the whole of the Earth above which He ruled.

The prayer was almost finished by the time the Inquisitor arrived to investigate. He had not shaved and his hair was unbrushed and uncovered, hanging over his ears to his collar. Nor was he fully dressed, and he held together the front of his coat at his chest.

He spoke to those he recognized, and to those who stood apart from the worshippers on their knees around the parson.

'Graven images,' an old man muttered as he passed by.

The Inquisitor looked up and wondered if he alone saw that the lines upon the hillside were neither smoothly cut in their gentle curves nor symmetrical in their design. One of them started twice as broad as it ended, whereas the others approximated some equal thickness along their full length; and one turned and then turned back upon itself, as though it had encountered some buried obstacle upon the hillside over which it had been unable to flow. He saw how little of the pattern had so far been revealed, and guessed that the overall design had been made too complicated and elaborate; that what had seemed straightforward and impressive on paper was going to prove difficult to achieve in these etched lines upon the bare white rock – a problem made no easier by the need to work so closely upon the hill and so far away from where the figure was intended to be seen and admired.

He saw the two veterans asleep against the wall of the church, filthy and exhausted after their night's labour. He never learned their names and thought of them only as Stump and Jaw, according to their injuries.

When the prayer was at last finished and the crowd rose to its feet, Jonas Webster came directly to join him.

'A pity our magistrate does not choose to share in our

praise. It is a good start. The Lord must now look down and be assured that we are firm in our conviction.' He stood with his back to the hillside.

'Your own wife,' the Inquisitor said. 'She too has been excluded.'

'A frail vessel.' He turned abruptly and walked away.

'The man must have his entrances and exits,' someone beside the Inquisitor said scornfully, but then he too turned and left before the Inquisitor could engage him in conversation.

Around him the others dispersed. Someone woke the sleeping veterans and was driven off by profanities. The hands, faces and clothing of these two men were white with chalk, making them appear, in the rising light, as though their skeletons had been crudely drawn upon them as they slept.

9

'You won't find her here.'

The Inquisitor stopped himself from turning. 'Oh?'

'No. Surely even you cannot have believed that here was where she was laid to rest.' There was mockery in Jonas Webster's voice. 'She will never rest. Never.'

'And are you so certain that I am looking for her?'

'That was why they never came back.'

'Who?'

'The old villagers. After the Death. You must have heard the tale of our Death.'

'They didn't come back because the new burial ground was never consecrated. Graves wherever they were dug.'

'Desperate remedies for desperate times.'

'If you say so.' The Inquisitor resumed his search of the small graveyard.

Finally conceding defeat, he turned back to the man.

'Then where?'

Jonas Webster nodded in the direction of the high land.

'At some crossroads?'

'In some blasted place where she might more easily be claimed by those she chose to worship.' He relished the remark.

And issuing from the mouth of your angel the warning to abandon all hope those who reject your own beneficent protection.

The man was a reader of minds for he stared hard at him.

'And the magistrate's wife?' the Inquisitor said.

'Taken by her parents and buried close by them. Likewise his daughters.'

'His daughters are dead also?' He had not been prepared for this.

'I assumed you knew. You and he are so often together.' He held out his open hand and then closed it finger by finger. 'The magistrate and the Inquisitor ranged against all the other poor ignorant souls here.'

'And are they buried in the same place?'

'Alongside their mother where they belong.'

'But why?'

The parson did not need to answer.

Were the woman's parents so disappointed in her choice of husband that they could deprive him even of the graves of his wife and daughters to kneel over?

'So they are all buried in—'

'That place. So I hear.'

'Are you there often? Have you visited the graves?'

'Why should I? They made clear their purpose in removing the bodies and he made clear his own in letting them go.'

'Then they all died here?'

'Within the year. I can tell you no more. Ask him.'

For a moment the Inquisitor believed that Samuel Mercer had joined them unseen and unheard, and that he had overheard all that had just passed between them. He felt as he had felt in the stonemason's yard – that the place was inhabited by some invisible presence.

'Church business,' Jonas Webster said. 'I visit the city only when I am obliged.'

And the only good thing to be said for the place was that it had rounded up and burned its Jews with more vigour than most. Rounded them up from the streets and surrounding villages, built its moat of God-fearing Christianity, driven them into the Round Tower, locked its heavy door on them, and then thrown in kindling and burning torches. Old men, women, and children, natural victims to the zealous excesses of any age. And those who did not burn or suffocate, but who survived amid the charred corpses of their families and friends, were offered their salvation by the Sick Beast contingent upon denouncing their god, their names, and their lives. And these last few were let out into the morning sunshine and the watching crowd gathered around the mound upon which the tower sat, and there they knelt and made their denunciations and pledges to the jeering of the onlookers, and there they were all beheaded and their heads carried on staves and hung from posts throughout the city.

For centuries no one leapt the moat, and those who had lost everything weighted their feet and stitched up their mouths and slid beneath its black waters, settling unseen and unmissed in the mud of abomination which coated its bottom.

'There were four names, four children.'

'Of what significance is it?' There was a colder edge than usual to the man's response.

'A son. Is he dead also?'

'Why ask all this of me? Ask the magistrate. Ask him. The sack upon my back of other men's sufferings and regrets is filled to overflowing. Do you think it gets any lighter with the passage of the years? Do you think every time a man is buried I can tip part of the load out upon his coffin? Ask him, not me.'

The Inquisitor continued surprised by the hostility which existed between the two men, and at the way this expressed itself – the one retreating within the core of silence at the heart of his own tragedy, and the other ready to spout these flames of denial and contempt at every opportunity.

52

But he did not then know of the terrible secret the two men shared, the secret as mortally destructive now as it had once been sustaining. Or if he did not know for certain of that secret, then he at least had some vague notion of it, and had guessed too that it was connected to the woman who had burned. He had also guessed that so consuming and destructive was this bond that even now, after the passage of over thirty years, each man lived in fear of some weakness in the other by which they might both be exposed. They were bound by it and yet kept apart by it, men not in chains but attached by an iron yoke which left them just beyond arm's reach, and which prevented others from coming between them.

The woman had burned and they had both in some way blackened their hands in throwing her to the flames.

'I intend visiting the site of the house,' the Inquisitor said, clearing his head of these tangled thoughts.

'To what end? There is nothing to see.'

'Oh?'

'The site was levelled, and everything retrievable taken away.'

'And was there much to take?' He hoped the man might contradict what the mason had already told him.

Jonas Webster said nothing.

He is fearful of my trap, thought the Inquisitor.

In the tall sere grass at the graveyard's edge there coughed a goatsucker, which then scuffled through the undergrowth to its burrow. Neither man saw the bird, but knew by its motions that it was bloated, wingless and blind.

'Could *you* show me where the woman is buried?'

Jonas Webster considered this, knowing that if he did not then someone else might. 'Perhaps when your work here is finished.'

'What do you know of the man who was said to live with

53

her before all this?' He knew of the man from the Commissioners' report, but had attached little significance to his presence.

'Questions, questions. Are we all so guilty? Are we all so openly accused? I answer only to the Lord.'

'So do we all. The man?'

'He was not of these parts. He came and he went.'

'Was he from the capital?' From as strange and distant a country as that?

'A foreigner.' The word was spoken in a near whisper. It might mean anything.

'From the Continent?'

Jonas Webster nodded.

'And so he was thought to be a plague carrier because that is where the plague – where all plagues – come from.'

No answer. Only the terrible bond. But he needed to see how far the light had penetrated into the darkness.

'One final question. Humour me. The magistrate's son, is he dead also?'

'Would that he were. He lived—'

'And his mother died in giving birth to him.'

'Such a choice for the Lord to make.'

'And where is he now? Does he associate with his father? Or can the man not bear to—'

'He associates with no one in this place.'

'And never visits?'

'Occasionally. He is a grown man. I believe he lives with his grandparents, or that they have some right of guardianship over him. He is, remember, their only acknowledged surviving heir.'

'Then they are still living?'

'I believe so. I know only that they took him, and that, alive or dead, they provide for him still.'

54

The enormity of this theft was greater than the Inquisitor could comprehend. 'Can all this be true?'

'Ask him, not me.'

The Inquisitor nodded, but knew, even before he raised his head to watch Jonas Webster walk away from him, that the questions were daggers primed for flesh, and he could not deny how firmly their handles fitted into his palm.

10

He saw Samuel Mercer from his window. A wind had risen and the magistrate stood with his hands thrust into his pockets. He looked up at the four white lines on the hillside as though they were that and nothing more. Several people passed him where he stood, and all stopped to speak with him.

There is a measure, a seasoning of pity, in everything that is said to him, thought the Inquisitor.

When he next looked out he saw that the magistrate was standing beneath his own window, and though his back was turned to the building, he knew the man wished to see him. He put down his pen, sealed the cap on his ink, and straightened his papers. He had filled sixty sheets since his arrival. He knew that his report to the Commissioners must be much shorter, and he could not explain, even to himself, why he wrote so copiously when his supply of materials was so precious and restricted, and when these excesses, should they ever be seen, would be denounced as both frivolous and misleading by the men to whom he was answerable.

A fire of peat and shavings kept his room warm, and although he could not deny the man outside, he regretted having to leave it on whatever errand he was being silently summoned to undertake.

Perhaps the magistrate wished to speak of the unspeakable and would tell him the story of his abandonment by all those he had once loved and cherished, the living and the dead alike. It was no part of why he, the Inquisitor, was there, but he acknowledged the interdependence of all things in that enclosed, self-regarding, and self-sufficient place, actions and words, rumour and plan, as woven together as individual threads within a piece of cloth upon which some matrix of colours and shapes had afterwards been stamped in pattern.

He went down into the street and made his meeting with the magistrate appear as though by accident.

'I hoped you might come.'

'Is there something you wish to discuss?'

'To show you.'

'Your angel?'

'No, although hereafter none of us will ever be able to avoid or ignore it. I dread most its eyes when it will look down on us and know us by everything we do in our most private places and everything we conjure up in our most private thoughts.'

'They may yet aspire to gaze into the kingdom of Heaven,' the Inquisitor said in encouragement.

'Have you seen the planned outline in its entirety?'

'No. Why?'

'I was wondering about its hands, wondering whether they might be praying for us, or pointing down to us in some more obvious gesture.'

The Inquisitor pulled on his gloves.

Together they left the village in the direction of the moor, but instead of climbing the road and passing the other men and women already on it, the magistrate led them up the slope at an angle so that they ascended along a more gentle path, invisible from below.

They emerged on the open moor half a mile distant from where the road gained the summit.

'I wish to show you our Aceldama,' the magistrate said.

The name was only distantly familiar to the Inquisitor.

'Our potter's field. More literally, the Field of Blood.'

The Inquisitor remembered. 'Land bought with the thirty pieces of silver given to Judas in payment for the betrayal of Christ.'

'Money deemed unlawful by the priests because it was the price of blood.'

'And the land was used only for the burial of strangers.'

'For the burial of those who would have no one to weep upon them where they knelt and clutched at the soil. Land which would provide no lasting comfort once that first great blade of grief had passed.'

They continued along the rim of the slope. Fires burned in the distance. The sky had brightened earlier, but was now the colour of pewter and filled with small dented clouds which added to that impression, gleaming occasionally where they scudded past the buried sun, but for the most part dull and slow.

The Inquisitor could think of nothing to say which might resume their conversation.

They walked until the village and the land surrounding it was lost to sight, and until they were above the canopy of the woodland which stretched endlessly away to the north.

Coming to a smooth stone set into the ground, the magistrate turned on to the moor.

They arrived soon afterwards at a depression, and dropping down into this the Inquisitor was surprised to see that, despite its shallowness, their heads did not come above it and that they were invisible to anyone upon the broader expanse of moor.

'Is this it?'

The magistrate pointed to the opposite edge of the

depression, where the Inquisitor, at first seeing nothing, was then able to make out three slight mounds, little more than ripples in the bowl of the ground.

'Not more secret graves, surely?' It seemed to him as though the entire geography of the district was made up more of these secret places with their whispered and feared associations than it was of features out in the open and upon a map to which a man might point and say without the slightest reservation: This, here, is where I live.

'They are no secret,' Samuel Mercer said.

The Inquisitor waited for an explanation.

'Three of Rupert's men were put to death here after the battle at Abwalton.'

'So far from the battlefield?'

'The story is that they were taken prisoner as they fled the carnage, coming to the high ground to seek refuge. They bargained for their lives with promises of a ransom. They were all wounded men and their journey was painful and slow.'

'And this is where their promises fell empty?'

'Or where the patience of their captors finally ran out. The men passed through the village and everyone there stayed in their homes lest the battle be brought to them. Some said they knew what was going to happen, why the three men had been brought to such an isolated place.'

'Did you see them?'

'No. I was away on business at the time. I returned, learned of what had happened, and came up here alone to discover if there was any substance to the stories.'

'And you found the bodies.'

'Where they lie now. Strangely, it was the first place I thought to look. The crows had been at them, and other scavengers. I argued for them to be removed to the churchyard, but to no avail. I could persuade only the father of the stonemason to come back up here with me and give them burial.'

'It was a dark time in the land,' said the Inquisitor, who had lost his own father at Worcester, and whose mother had died riven with sorrow six months later.

They stood together, unseen, with the wind purling above them, and said a prayer for the slain men.

PART II

11

Leaves fell from their trees at the height of a long summer and formed themselves into strange and secret symbols on the ground; crops grew in full appearance of being rich and healthy and then their grains and seeds and pods burst in clouds of poisonous black spores; a gentle mare threw her owner and then danced upon him with her forelegs raised up in the air as though supported by some invisible partner until he was battered and bloody, and later died; one year bees fed on a sweet dunghill and their honey stank, the next year the hives were opened to find that they had been invaded by wasps; in the city twin girls were born joined by a fleshy channel which stretched in a fifth unnatural breast between them and through which their shared blood could be seen flowing; in the church-yard a company of cats gathered to dig up the body of a recently buried child; the river shrank and fish climbed out upon its banks in search of another; blood appeared in the pails of milked cows and pus flowed from the teats of nursing women; on even the stillest of days clouds formed themselves into the shapes of beasts and men, and when darkness came the heavens were criss-crossed with burning stars which flew from one end of the night to the other, neither vanishing nor diminishing in brilliance as they went.

Samuel Mercer fell limp in his seat. He had rehearsed this litany and was grateful that the man to whom he had recited it had not interrupted him – either to question him upon specifics or to prod him with the scepticism he felt certain he must feel. He gripped the arms of his chair, as though bracing himself against the questions which he knew must now surely follow.

For his part, the Inquisitor weighed up the man before him, knowing that any direct dismissal of what he had just been told might cause him to retreat even further into the unassailable void he so clearly craved. He knew by the dull monotone of the magistrate's voice that he was merely repeating what countless others might afterwards be pressed into telling him.

He had with him the Commissioners' map of the land upon which the house had once stood. His visit that evening had been concerned with particular details of this, but he knew now that their discussion must remain rooted in this contentious mulch.

'And for all this she was called a witch and burned?'

'For this she was called a witch.'

Neither man, in his own cautious way, gave the accusation much credence.

'And burned?'

'No; I believe that was accidental.' Samuel Mercer turned away, pretending to rake a fire which did not need raking, and which spat out flakes of glowing wood into the hearth.

'What other charges were brought against her?'

'These were not charges, merely accusations.'

'But which nevertheless were ultimately responsible for her death, accidental or otherwise.'

The magistrate nodded.

'A brazen head was burned upon her door.' He slid open a drawer in the small chest beside him, and without looking into it he withdrew a sheet of paper and handed it to the Inquisitor. It contained a sketch of the brazen head.

'You drew this?'

'I did.'

He could not ask if it were record or design and he handed it back without any further comment on it. Samuel Mercer put the sheet back into the drawer and slid it shut.

Then the Inquisitor unrolled his map and pinned it flat with books upon the table. Samuel Mercer glanced at it and a slight involuntary spasm appeared to pass through him.

'Do you recognize it?'

'I believe now that she was persecuted unjustly.'

'And the chorus of condemnation that rose up against her?'

'That, regrettably, it grew beyond the control of reason and informed judgement. People copied others. They saw that they were losing their livelihoods and sought to attach blame to someone.'

'And there was no suggestion that all these occurrences might have had some natural cause?'

'Do you suggest that they were visited upon us by the Almighty?'

'That is how some might have chosen to view them.'

The magistrate shook his head. 'His servant here filled every breach.'

'Then Jonas Webster too was vociferous against the woman?'

Again the magistrate nodded, as though this were somehow less than saying the word, as though it kept him at a distance from the events thus described, apart from all the resurrected and undeniable connections and allegiances so easily made.

Conscious of this, the Inquisitor turned back to his map. 'There is mention here of a well.' He smoothed out creases and sought with his forefinger.

'There was a well.'

The Inquisitor sat back from the map, inviting the other to lean forward and identify it. But the man did not move, did not even raise his eyes from his lap where his clasped hands grew tight and pale.

'And was this also destroyed when the house was burned?'

Samuel Mercer could not bring himself to speak.

A good and reliable well in that place would have been a precious thing. The moors were a sponge, and the water of the sluggish rivers in the Vale pestilential.

'Is it shown?' the magistrate asked, his eyes still down, the three words no more than a painful whisper.

'No. Only named somewhere in the vicinity of the house.'

'Then it is lost. And useless. No one will build there or live there until the memory of that place is completely forgotten.'

The Inquisitor resisted asking how long he believed this might be. The answer could only be until everyone now living there died and then their children died after them, whereupon the facts of the matter – confused and unsubstantiated as these already were – might enter into the less harmful realm of cautionary tale and myth.

'Do you still intend to visit the site?'

It was another of the reasons for the Inquisitor's visit that evening, but even though now prompted he did not say so; nor did he ask for the magistrate to accompany him as he had intended.

He had set out to examine the place two days earlier, but had been forced back by a sudden heavy downpour which turned his path through the woodland into a river of mud.

There was a third reason for his visit.

'Who was the man who lived with her? I know only that he was a stranger to this place and that he left soon before she was killed. Was he another of her accusers? Or was he driven off so that he might not act as witness to what was to happen to her?'

66

Only this last remark stung Samuel Mercer into response.

'How so? I told you, none of it was planned. How would we know to drive him off? He simply left. He came and he went.'

'From a place where the plague was already established? Was he fleeing this? Did he bring it here with him?'

The magistrate half rose from his seat and banged his fist on the table.

'No, no. If he had been suffering from the sickness he would not have been allowed to come so far or so close.'

But the Inquisitor could not release his grip on the matter. 'Perhaps he travelled by night and hid himself during the day. Perhaps he was some relative or friend of the woman and he came to her because he knew she would take pity on him and nurse him. He might even have been—'

'He was a Dutchman,' Samuel Mercer shouted, again slapping the table before falling back into his seat.

The Inquisitor sat silenced.

'Why did no one tell me?'

The magistrate could not speak.

'Then he was a mercenary come over in the service of the King. Is that it? Was he wounded at some lost battle and then found his way here and to the woman's house? She nursed him and it was the final straw heaped upon the camel's back. He was driven away to die or recover elsewhere and the people of the village exacted their punishment upon her.'

The magistrate held out his palms to the fire.

The Inquisitor rolled up his map.

'Is it such a terrible revelation?' he asked.

'Perhaps not for you,' the magistrate said.

They sat together like two men who had collided in the moonless night and had then withdrawn, neither seeing the other but aware now that he was no longer alone, and that he was being sought in the darkness.

67

'A man here, in the village, was struck by a thunderbolt from the heavens.'

'And is that so strange?'

'There was neither rain nor wind. There was no cloud nor any other disturbance so that we might know it was coming. A peaceful summer's day and he was struck.'

'And did he survive?'

'He is living still.'

'Here?'

The magistrate nodded.

'Will you point him out to me? Does he still bear the scars?'

'He does. But if he wishes to reveal himself to you then it must be of his own accord.'

'And was this, like the Dutchman, too much to bear after all your other misfortunes?'

There was more.

'A child was born malformed. This, I believe, is what incited the assault.'

The sudden and penetrating light of understanding shines no less fiercely upon acts and arguments founded in stupidity and ignorance than it does upon those born of reason and intellect.

'The woman was at one time our midwife, you see. Two of my own daughters she delivered in perfect safety, with ill effects to neither my wife nor the girls themselves.'

'And knowing this you could do nothing to save her?'

For the first time the magistrate's eyes looked directly into the Inquisitor's. 'Do you truly need to ask that of me?'

The Inquisitor apologized. It was beyond him now to ask the man to accompany him the following day.

12

His visit disappointed him. There was nothing to see and no sense to make of the markings on his map. He had expected too much. Thirty years had passed. Young trees had grown mature, old trees had fallen and rotted, and all that remained was the overgrown trace of the path which had once led through the woodland from the village, and which was dark beneath the autumn canopy, though occasionally flush with new growth, now dying, where there had been some clearance and sunlight had fallen to the ground.

The maps of the Commissioners were maps of property and boundaries, of tithe disputes and valuations; they were not the maps of unknown spaces, of oceans and lands dotted here and there with fishes and mythical beasts. They were not the maps of dreamers and adventurers, but the maps of men who walked the bounds between fields and knew that to their right the land was worth seven pence a rod and that to their left only six.

He followed the path for an hour and then stopped, believing he had come too far. He was about to inspect his map when he heard voices in the trees ahead of him. He fell silent – he had been singing to himself – and stepped off the path until he was hidden amid an overgrown coppice. The voices continued: talking, a brief silence, and then laughter. And so distorted were these sounds by the obstacles through which

69

they came to him that it seemed as though he were hearing a returning echo rather than the voices themselves. He listened intently, straining for every sound, but still he could not identify the talkers.

He stepped back out on to the path and continued walking. The voices stopped, and he feared he had been seen and was now being observed. He watched where he placed his feet, careful not to step on any dead branch. In places the path was still flooded and his boots were heavy with mud.

Someone called for him to stop, and he instinctively raised his hand to protect himself before lowering it and calling for whoever had shouted to reveal himself.

The two veterans stepped on to the path ahead of him. Each held a clay jug and they came towards him.

'It is our judge,' said the man with the missing leg.

'We have but one true judge,' said the other, his spilled words barely comprehensible. They burst into laughter.

When they were again composed, the first said, 'Aye, but the parson is a fair-paying man for all that.' Their laughter resumed. They were drunk, and the Inquisitor saw this by the way they waved their jugs at him and slopped the drink on their clothes.

'I don't think our two judges care overmuch for each other,' Stump said provocatively.

'Be that as it may,' said the Inquisitor.

Jaw repeated this in a mocking tone. He slavered and wiped his mouth on his sleeve.

The Inquisitor went to pass them, but the men blocked his path, and on either side of where they stood he saw only cushions of saturated moss. To get by them he would have to retreat.

'What do you think to our work on the hill?' Jaw asked him.

70

'I see that it takes shape.'

'He sees that it takes shape.'

He was not accustomed to insolence, but knew that his authority was no threat to the two men.

'He will have wings,' Stump said, raising his arms.

'Aye, and a look of such scorn that all men who come here will be struck dumb in awe of him.'

Such eloquence surprised the Inquisitor until he understood that the man was merely repeating what Jonas Webster had said to him perhaps a hundred times.

The angel had grown but little since the staged revelation of its first few lines. Avarice and vanity destroyed what they created. He grew angry at the continued provocation of the two men.

'But supposing what you drew upon that hill were one of Peter's fallen angels,' he said.

'We don't draw it, Judge. We cut and scrape it out by the sweat of our brows and the labour of our backs.'

The two men shared a nervous glance.

'Excuses. Supposing it were an angel of the Second Epistle.' He took pleasure in confounding them even further.

'Ask the parson,' Jaw said, moving to stand closer to Stump.

'False prophets and false teachers denigrating the words of the Lord and speaking of damnable heresies to bring upon themselves some swift and all-consuming destruction.'

'It is an angel, mute though all-seeing.'

'What else do you remember to spout?'

Stump raised his fist, but thought better of the threat and lowered it.

'God spared not the angels that sinned but cast them down to hell and delivered them into chains of darkness to be reserved unto judgement.'

71

Neither man could find the words to answer him. Jaw panted wetly in anger; Stump raised his jug to his lips and then swore when he found it empty.

The Inquisitor surprised himself at having remembered so much. The reading was not accurate, but accurate enough in its essentials. His mind was concentrated.

'Stand aside,' he said, tightening his grip on his staff.

'He's going to the house.'

'Oh? I was led to believe there was nothing there to see.'

'Does the parson know?'

'What business is it of his?'

'No one here ever visits the place.'

Stump told Jaw to shut up.

'And yet you two are close enough to it now.'

Neither man denied this and their silence reassured and encouraged him. He took several paces towards them and they stepped off the path for him to pass. They sank to their shins in the wet ground, but neither seemed to notice or to care.

He walked away from them expecting to hear them call after him, but nothing came.

He arrived at his destination several minutes later. It was no more than a clearing in the surrounding woodland, already overgrown and long returned to the wild. Of the house there was nothing, merely the suggestion of a raised mound. He prodded at this but found nothing.

His search lasted only a few minutes, after which he could not even convince himself that he was at the right place. But the Commissioners would enquire after the condition of the site and now he would be able to satisfy them.

It was late afternoon when he left, and he was grateful to go.

Returning along the same path, and knowing by the falling sun that night would soon come, he found himself running, finally stopping to catch his breath when he unexpectedly emerged into the open alongside the churchyard, and where he saw that he was being watched.

The three men stood together by the church door, and upon his appearance they parted. Jonas Webster entered the church and the two others turned a corner and were lost to him.

It was a long time since he had run so far or with such urgency, and he leaned forward, his hands on his knees, until the ache in his ribs was gone. Frothy phlegm fell from his lips on to the leaves at his feet, and he spat out more before searching for a handkerchief and wiping his lips.

13

News from the Commissioners' agent reached him the next day.

It was mid-morning and he had been risen only a few minutes when he saw through the gap of his shuttered windows Jonas Webster's wife coming along the street. The woman lived in the cold and unsustaining shadow of her husband. She was governed by him, and he pitied her. Like his labourers, she repeated only what her husband had said before her, and even when pressed for her own opinion upon some matter gave answers which, their hesitancy apart, were indistinguishable from his own. She was seldom in the company of others in the village, and even less frequently without Jonas Webster somewhere within watching or hailing distance. He was her anchor and rudder, and without him she was a vessel at the mercy of every wind and tide.

Of all this, the Inquisitor was shortly to be disabused.

He watched her approach, and something in the way she came, her head down except for her glances to where he stood unseen and watched her, told him that her errand was to him.

She wore a shawl and a hood, and whenever the wind tugged this from her head she immediately pulled it back.

She was stopped directly beneath his window by an older woman who held up her basket to reveal its contents. He

74

guessed by the way their voices were raised and their hands waved that the old woman was offering something for sale, which Jonas Webster's wife did not wish to buy. Had she been her husband she would have passed the old woman without a word.

He saw how uncomfortable she was, how exposed. The old woman grabbed her arm; others gathered to participate in the encounter.

The Inquisitor watched all this intently. He took no personal satisfaction in the woman's discomfort, but shared vicariously in the mean enjoyment of the villagers who surrounded her.

He began to cough, and so withdrew from where he might be heard by those below.

He had retired to his bed at eight the previous evening and had woken at two with a fever. He perspired heavily and opened the small window to let in the chill night air. He fell briefly back to sleep and then woke again, this time shivering. He attributed his discomfort to his exertions of the previous day. He carried with him a variety of potions and he diluted and drank several of these. The rest of the night remained sleepless, and it was not until the late dawn that he was finally able to rest. It was because of this that he had remained in his bed so late.

He washed and dressed. His hair was grown too long and he intended later that day to seek out a barber and have it cut.

In truth, he had grown discontented with his work there, and this was made worse by his uncertainty as to how to proceed and what was now expected of him.

The landlord knocked and said that the woman was downstairs asking to see him. The rooms below were cold, and having built up his own fire the Inquisitor told the man to ask her to come up.

'She'll be unwilling to do that, sir.'

'Then insist. We humour her husband often enough, fall silent when he speaks, obey *his* commands. Well, she is not he.'

'Sir.' The landlord withdrew and through the closed door the Inquisitor heard him practising what he would say to the woman.

She appeared fifteen minutes later.

He invited her in and placed a chair by the fire for her. The draw on the chimney had sucked most of the rank smell of sleep from the small room and he left open the window to clear it further.

At first she was reluctant to sit down, as though this simple act committed her to something more.

'They gather like geese at a prowling cat,' he said, looking down at the women still outside. They were leaves blown in a drift and would remain where they stood until some other gust of news or gossip settled them elsewhere.

The woman unfastened her hood, and as she slid off her cape the Inquisitor saw fastened around her neck a small crampball, which she immediately tucked back inside her collar as it swung free.

'They despise my company, and I theirs,' she said.

'Not a particularly charitable attitude for one so closely attached to the Lord's servant among them.' He smiled at her so that she might not misinterpret his true meaning.

She shrugged, and in that instant he saw in her a spirit he would not have believed existed from their meetings in the company of her husband, and he knew then that his pity, or sympathy, whichever he felt, was misplaced.

'He is no more *their* servant than I am.'

'Then are they yours?'

She paused in thought, drew off her gloves and held her hands to the fire. 'I do not intend to be trapped by your clever words. I brought you this.' She took a sealed letter from her sleeve, and the sight of it made the Inquisitor immediately anxious as to its contents. It was even possible that he would be recalled to the capital. He resisted the urge to snatch it from her and she laid it on the stool between them.

They were interrupted by the return of the landlord, who carried in a tray of warm cordial. He was nervous in their presence and came no closer than the table upon which he set down the drink. The Inquisitor thanked him and he left.

'It came to us by a pedlar who makes it part of his business to carry communications. It might have been weeks coming here. The man comes from the swamps of Holderness to the moor on his way to the Vale. It is addressed to you care of my husband. Perhaps your masters expected you to find lodging with us.'

'It is common practice elsewhere.'

'I see. A pity, then.'

He did not ask her to explain, and it was only much later, when the time came for him to leave, and when he would for ever afterwards curse and damn the place in his prayers and dreams, that he regretted not having made an ally of the woman. Admittedly, she was Janus-faced, with a face for him, one for her husband, and yet another for the villagers, but she was also cautious and surreptitious where her husband was blind and forceful; and she knew when to fall silent and disappear behind him when he knew only to rage and threaten. What the Inquisitor had hitherto regarded as fearful subservience he now saw as something else entirely.

She took her drink and studied the room around her.

'You have few comforts,' she said.

'I need few. I take comfort from my work.'

It was a glib remark, neither wholly true nor false, and she saw this but did not pursue it.

'Are you not going to read your letter? Or do you fear I am as loose-tongued as those outside?'

'I imagine they are at work on it already.'

'I concealed it from them, but the pedlar will no doubt be selling his useless wares on the strength of it. It is always good to have a firm reason for coming here.' She looked at him pointedly as she said this.

'And another for leaving?'

She emptied her cup and rose.

Their encounter was over and the advantage remained with her.

'You suffer from the cramps?' he said to her, a final unjust prod while her back was turned.

She hesitated before answering. 'I suffer from the superstitions of those around me. I suffer from neighbours who still stuff their small cuts with cobwebs and who gather spiders for the ague. We were always thus.'

Unexpectedly, the Inquisitor started to cough again, holding a cloth to his mouth until the violent spasm was over. Tears formed uncontrollably in his eyes.

She waited until he was composed and then left him. In a gesture of reciprocal kindness he offered to walk with her back to her home, but she declined this and let herself out.

He went to the chair she had vacated by the fire, taking with him a blanket to wrap around his feet.

The letter from the Commissioners disappointed him. Why had they not heard sooner from him? Another report on property only three parishes distant had spoken of steeply rising yields and profits from the newly drained land. Why was the damaged property – he laughed aloud at the word – not repaired and put back into good working order so that a similar advantage might be taken of the land attached to it? A new map was required, the old one being clearly out of date and useless for their purpose. Finally, it was suggested that if money was to be saved then he might consider moving into any part of the property still inhabitable and making it secure. They sent him God's protection. He threw down the single sheet and stamped his foot on it. They had no idea. They expected too much. They had sent him on a fool's errand.

When his anger had subsided he retrieved the letter and read on.

He was to ignore anything he might be told about the circumstances in which the property had been abandoned, and concentrate solely on how it might now be brought back into profitable use. Here was the reassuring yet illusory light of rescue flashed from the shore to a foundering boat.

In the past he had relished his work in isolation. He had no family to miss him during his long absences, and he had enjoyed travelling to distant places and adding to his knowledge of the country as he went. But never before had he felt himself so distant from any centre as he felt himself now. And never before had he felt so alone, so deprived of the new company to which he usually moored himself while he worked. He might die there and be buried there, his maps and papers along with him, and his headstone might be the only mark he left upon the world.

He tried to rid his mind of these morbid thoughts, but later in the day his fever returned and he again retired early to his bed, where he slept a sleep of fitful interruption, part dream and part restless waking for the remainder of the day and the whole of the following night.

14

A man from the village went missing and was found drowned two days later, pulled from a pool on the river known to be the resting place of all its weightier flotsam. He was lifted out amid a tangle of rotten boughs, the bones of long-dead animals, and liquefying fleeces, and carried back to his grieving mother on a litter. There was a large bruise on his stomach, swollen and discoloured, and some said he had been kicked by a stray cow or shod horse into the water, where he had lain unconscious while it filled his lungs.

It surprised some that he was found so far from where he had last been seen working. The river had not been in spate since the previous winter's melt, and nor was it deep enough along any of its intervening stretches to have floated him to the pool without stranding him sooner upon some gravel bank or leaving him trapped by a limb amid exposed roots or one of its reed beds.

The stonemason carried him the final mile back to the village. His daughter had been going to wed the man the following year, and she walked beside her father crying as she came, frequently rushing to him to cradle her dead lover's head and to kiss him on his bloodless lips and cheeks. Her father tried to keep her away. The body was loose in his arms and he paused before entering the village to secure the man's clothes and to hold him as straight as possible across his forearms. He tried to persuade his daughter to compose herself, but she was unable to, and her wailing rose in pitch and grew continuous as she tried helplessly to expel the grief already burrowing so deep inside her suddenly empty body.

Others came and offered to relieve the man of his burden, but the mason refused. Women tried to console his daughter, but she fought off their sympathy with her fists. Finally entering her father's yard, she held one of the dead man's hands in both her own, and when the mason finally laid him down on a granite slab in the shadow of his tallest angel, she fell beside him, pressed herself to him and cried unceasingly into his dead face.

The stonemason stood back from her, embarrassed by her actions, but knowing it was beyond him to grasp her shoulders and lead her gently away. She had pulled the man's shirt from his belt and the bruise showed up vividly in the hollow of his stomach.

His mother arrived and she too fell beside the body and began loudly mourning. Neither woman consoled the other, and neither sought consolation in this shared outpouring of their grief.

The magistrate came, and with him the Inquisitor. Samuel Mercer had a perfunctory duty to perform and asked the stonemason where the body had been found. He then spoke to the man who had last seen him alive. This was the extent of his involvement. He did not concern himself with speculation on how the man had died, or when. He approached no closer than ten feet of the corpse and the women bent over it, each reclaiming as forcefully as she knew how some part of it or some memory of it. The dead man's head rested between the feet of the angel, and the shadow of its praying hands fell across his closed eyes.

'How old was he?' the Inquisitor asked the mason.

'Nineteen. His mother is widowed and he is the last of her children.'

Jonas Webster arrived and was immediately approached by the mason who asked if he could get his daughter to withdraw. She was by then as wet as the man on the ground, and her hair lay plastered in clouts across her face. So great and prolonged was her crying that her throat had dried and she had lost her voice, and to those who could not see her, but who waited outside the yard and heard her, her convulsive sobbing sounded more like the cries of an alarmed animal than a woman speechless in her distress.

'Was he kicked?' Jonas Webster asked the mason. There was little concern in his voice, and he looked with distaste at the angel as he spoke.

'It might just be a mark caused by the rolling of the water. Do you have a coffin in the church?'

Jonas Webster did not answer. 'Why does your own daughter grieve so?'

'She and he were to be wed. Surely you cannot have forgotten.'

Watching this exchange, the Inquisitor believed the mason capable of grabbing Jonas Webster and demanding that he acknowledge his daughter's grief and that the body be removed to the sanctuary of the church. And this he would do more for himself and his child than for the dead man and his mother.

'I vaguely remember them coming to see me,' Jonas Webster said. 'A great pity. We can ill afford to lose such youth and strength.' This time he looked at the girl as he spoke. Then he walked away, leaving the mason unable to call after him.

Eventually the man could bear the inhuman convulsions of his daughter no longer and he went to her and pulled her roughly away from the corpse. But she clung to the body and the dead man's shirt was rent in her hands. She was beaten off too by the man's mother, and she cursed her and her father both as she was carried away by him, beating upon his back and head as he took her through the parting crowd and into her home. He kicked shut the door behind him, but her cries and raving could be heard for long afterwards through the walls.

And they were heard every day and night of the week that followed, after which she fell silent.

At the end of her ordeal she reappeared and took her place among the other women. She was exhausted and said little, and in appearance seemed to have doubled in age, having forsaken or sacrificed her young married life and the prospect of motherhood as she knelt and wept in her father's yard.

The Inquisitor saw her afterwards in the fields, and on one occasion on the moor, but whenever they met she refused to speak to him. He told her how sorry he was, told her he spoke from experience, but her ears were deaf to everything he said and her eyes looked at him unblinkingly as though he were not there, and as though all she could see was something beyond the distant horizon, invisible to everyone except herself.

He watched her working, as she cut and tied and stacked mechanically, little caring how well she completed her tasks. None of the other women intervened. When they rested she sat apart from them, and the Inquisitor saw by the glances and the hushed conversation of these others that they expected her grief to force itself back to the surface and begin anew to extort its toll on her.

There was further speculation on how the man had died. Some suggested that he had been visiting another woman, and that this accounted for his great distance from the village; others, no less cruelly, said he was leaving the place for good, that he had confided this to some but not to the mason's daughter. And some made guesses wild and unbelievable, accepted or dismissed in accordance with the listener's feelings towards the man and the girl before his death.

The Inquisitor found it hard to understand why so little comfort was offered to the girl, why people shunned her instead of surrounding and supporting her in her need. It struck him afterwards as a peculiar characteristic of the place and its inhabitants, and he would remember this cold charity as long as he lived.

The man was buried four days after he was found. It rained into his open grave. His mother kept up her daily vigil, but the mason's daughter never once went into the churchyard, and was for ever afterwards absent from the church itself.

15

The Inquisitor compiled his report. In the eyes of the Commissioners he had thus far achieved nothing. It was a useless task, tainted by acrimony, and one at which an army of surveyors and land agents would fail just as fully as he. He began to wonder if there had been some other reason for sending him this far and upon such a useless errand, but concluded that he was overreacting, that although his body might have recovered to health, his mind had not yet shaken off the last of its delirium. He was neither tried nor persecuted, and as if to convince himself more fully of this, he copied the words into his journal. He also wrote – and the thought had long since occurred to him – that just as he had never before felt so alone in his work, or so distant from some sustaining core, so he had never before come upon a place so precariously balanced between the twin attractions and repulsions of Heaven and Hell. He was unable to explain this feeling any more accurately, but it was a powerful impression and one he could not dismiss. Later, when he put this notion to Samuel Mercer, the magistrate let him know that he too concurred in the belief, but would be drawn no further, remarking merely that they lived in a time and a place more attuned to the demands of justice than of mercy. The solemnity of this reply puzzled the Inquisitor, but he did not pursue it. Silences were pierced by distant noises, largely unheard, and emptinesses were filled from within.

He returned to the site of the house.

Midway along his journey through the woodland he came upon a tree which had fallen across his path, and through which he had to force a passage. His sleeves and hair became entangled and he was able to extricate himself only with caution and pain.

Having surmounted this obstacle, he rested, tired by his exertions and deceived by his apparent recovery. He carried a satchel of papers, pens, and measures, intent upon redrawing the immediate vicinity of the lost house. This new map would allow him to dispense with the misleading charts upon which the Commissioners fixed their hope and expectation – both so firmly that they might have been translated into symbols and plotted on the grid. But whatever he achieved would ultimately disappoint, ink spilled on a page of perfect manuscript.

One of the fastenings on his satchel was torn during his struggle through the fallen tree and he tried unsuccessfully to repair this before going on. Later, he found that he had lost one of his precious mapping pens and he called out to threaten the spirit of the place which had taken it from him.

There was little birdsong in the woodland, perhaps silenced by his presence, and few indications of the rabbits which swarmed elsewhere over the farmland and moors, and which were killed in great numbers. Only the previous afternoon he had watched the burning of a field of stubble and had seen the boys and men of the village drive the flames towards the centre of the enclosed space, circling with slings and sticks and waiting for the animals herded there to dash free. Most of these they killed, yelling and gesticulating as they ran from one confused and terrified creature to another, leaving them dead or wounded and writhing on the scorched ground as they turned to their next target. Some of the rabbits waited so long amid their diminishing patch of cover that when they finally did dash out into the open the fur of their backs was smouldering in the heat, and some were so blinded by their pain that they ran either into the flames or directly into the legs of the men waiting to kill them. Afterwards almost two hundred carcasses had been gathered and stacked into a soft and twitching mound.

The site was as he had left it.

He cleared a space for himself upon another fallen trunk and took out his maps, turning them one way and then another until he believed he had aligned them correctly to the ground before him, confounded by both their misleading simplicity and unnecessary elaborations.

He saw where the house had once stood, and believed now that he could discern some vague outline of connecting walls beneath the mound. But on this occasion his attention lay elsewhere, and he sought instead for the well, knowing that if this source of fresh water could be found then it alone might act as some impetus for rebuilding, thus turning the land back to profitable use. Without it the site would remain as worthless as that surrounding it and would undoubtedly be left untended to the rank encroachment of the trees.

There was no exact mark, only the letters, and from these he deduced a site twenty feet distant from the house. Standing at the centre of this guessed location he drove in a stick, attached a cord measure, and marked out a circle. He slashed at the undergrowth within this and then began to probe beneath.

He searched for an hour to no avail, but then he pressed in his stave and felt it pass unresisting to a depth of two feet. He tried close by and felt the same. He regretted that he had not brought a spade with him. He dug with his hands, pulling up the weeds and saplings which had rooted there. Then he prised up the loose surface with a stouter branch. There was still no shape on the ground, and no indication of anything buried beneath, but he was convinced by the texture of the soil that he was searching in the right place.

He quickly exhausted himself, and after a further half an hour had found nothing. His hands and forearms were black and scratched, and he felt blood beneath the dirt. In addition to the spade, he now regretted that he had not thought to bring the gauntlets which might protect his hands.

Then he uncovered a piece of brick, a broken corner ⌐rmed into a small pyramid, and he rejoiced as though it were buried treasure, and a moment later found the rest of the clay block intact.

He studied the hollow from which he had pulled this and then poked into the soil on either side of it. There were two more bricks, and beyond these two others, curving slightly, and then two more and two more and two more until a definite half-circle was revealed to him. He measured this and found it to be three feet in diameter. He had uncovered the rim of the well. Any part of the structure which might once have risen above the level of the ground had been demolished, possibly tipped into the bore itself. He probed and found more broken brick-work. Like a man able to see around corners, he was correct in every guess he made. He rose elated and went back to the mound where the house had stood and looked down on his discovery. And for the first time he saw things as they might once have been. History and geography he uncovered with every scoop of his palm. And he felt that history and geography acutely, as though it were a vision, a reward for his perseverance.

He retrieved several pieces of the broken brick and cleaned them with a tiny besom of twigs. They were compact and heavy for their size, and some contained strips of the mortar which had once bound them together. This too was of high quality and he was convinced that the well had not collapsed of its own accord. There was nothing of comparable construction elsewhere in the village.

He returned to his lodgings, passing men and women in the street and fields but telling no one of what he had found. Some, he believed, saw it in his face and in his stride and did not need to be told. He passed the stoneyard and saw the mason at work, raining blow after blow upon an ungiving slab of rock as though it were his mortal enemy. There seemed to be little method in this assault, and the Inquisitor did not pause to speak to him. A ghost of dust rose high above the man and shimmered in the breeze like blown silk.

16

It rained heavily through the night and into the following day, and when this finally ceased it was too late for him to return to the well and so he spent his time going from house to house in the hope of finding two or three others to assist him. Everywhere he asked he met with refusal. And where the men were not at home their wives answered for them.

He called on Samuel Mercer to see if he would intervene on his behalf, or, failing this, if he might lend him the necessary tools to continue the work himself. But there was no answer to his summons, and he came away even more frustrated.

The rain stopped falling and he climbed the road to the moor.

Work on the angel had progressed only slowly, and though the outline of the head and arms and wings was now sketched in the chalk, there was nothing to equal the miracle of those first few lines.

There were men working on the hillside now, and at the foot of the slope he saw Jonas Webster directing them. The parson shouted until he was hoarse, exasperated by the lack of understanding between himself and his labourers, by their sloth and their unwillingness to keep to the narrow paths he had marked for them outside the design. Spoil heaps were dotted around the figure and white blemishes had appeared which were no part of the angel. In places the thin crust of turf had been disturbed, and where this had happened it was washed away by the rain. Something which had started life as the most perfect and assured of visions was becoming like all things human, imperfect, succumbing to uncontrollable forces and prey to misunderstanding, and Jonas Webster felt the unwanted marks and lines upon the hillside as though they were scars cut into his flesh.

The men who laboured were grey with the sludge of chalk and soil and their discontent showed in everything they did.

Jonas Webster looked up and saw the Inquisitor, and he immediately fell silent and withdrew.

'You are witness to his waking dream turned nightmare.'

The voice startled him and he turned to see the stone-mason. He had come over the brow of the hill from the moor and was carrying a bundle of roots. His daughter stood dark-eyed and silent beside him.

'I wonder he works in these conditions at all,' the Inquisitor said. He watched the girl and saw how far she had retreated from her own life into the abyss of her loss.

'He doesn't. He finds others to do it for him. Like a general directing his troops from some safe place overlooking the field of battle. The more numerous his workers, the greater his range of excuses.'

From where they stood they could see other imperfections in the design, curves and lines and angles which did not work in accord with the flow of the contours upon which they were drawn.

'Whatever becomes of it, it will be no relief for our sufferings.' The mason glanced at his daughter, as close yet as insubstantial as his shadow. He spoke as though she were not present. All three of them knew that the suffering and endurance of bereavement was never divided into smaller shares among those forced to bear it, only multiplied by that same

91

number. The mason had adopted a policy of containment, and the persistent weight upon his own back was now double that which had so easily and swiftly crushed his daughter. She was all he had, and the Inquisitor wondered if he woke in the night and went full of dread to ensure that she too had not been lost to him.

They parted and the girl followed her father without even the slightest acknowledgement that the encounter had taken place.

The Inquisitor turned his face to the east and immediately felt the wind that blew from that direction. Those who worked on the moor said they could taste in it the salt from the distant sea.

The women were at work amid the bracken and he approached where they stood. In the absence of the girl they spoke to him and encouraged his conversation. They knew of his discovery and search for help, but both he and they alike made no mention of this. They expressed their fears for the girl and her father, and spoke of their own urgency now that the cold and wet of autumn had fully arrived. They spoke of the season as though it had been sent with the sole purpose of working against them, chiding them into readiness for the one which was to follow. And when they spoke of winter it was with a mixture of caution, reverence, and fear, as though a great leaden dome were about to be placed over them, from which they might somehow not be released the following spring.

He left them and continued walking, and on the first occasion he lifted his eyes to trace the road ahead of him, he saw a horseman approaching. The man drew close and reined in his mount, and as the Inquisitor went to greet him he dismounted.

He was a well-dressed man, with a wig beneath his hat.

He dripped from head to foot where he had been caught in the rain but seemed little concerned by his obvious discomfort. At the Inquisitor's approach he held out his hand.

'You, I imagine, are the Church Commissioner.'

'Merely their servant,' the Inquisitor told him, having briefly savoured the title which might one day be his own. 'How do you know of me?'

The man laughed. 'The same way everyone else within a twenty-mile radius of the place knows of you. I believe they call you their Inquisitor. No wonder they live in awe of you.'

The Inquisitor was confused by the answer and the man saw this.

'My apologies. John Colley. A friend of Lord Kepwick, on my way to visit him now at Kepwick Hall.'

'I don't know the place.'

'But heard of it, surely?'

The Inquisitor shook his head.

'Five miles distant from you in the village. North. Pass through the woodland and you pass through the boundary of the estate. The hall lies beyond a spur of the moor which separates you.' He lifted the hoof of his mount and inspected it.

The Inquisitor felt uncomfortable in his ignorance.

'I'm afraid the villagers regard the place with some suspicion, scorn even,' John Colley said. 'The original site of the village was once on the estate before its boundaries contracted. It was abandoned centuries ago and one of Kepwick's ancestors had the remains carted away.' He spoke as though the event were of no consequence, but the Inquisitor saw immediately why the place had not been mentioned to him.

'The plague,' he said.

'I believe so. The people and their dwellings were an affront to his – what shall we call it? – sensibility, and so when

93

the opportunity arose he did something about them both. When the survivors came back down out of hiding it was to find their homes gone and themselves dispossessed.'

'And this bad feeling, this lack of contact, has persisted for three hundred and fifty years?'

'Why not? Suspicion and hatred breed suspicion and hatred.' Colley looked around him. 'Did you know that it was one of Kepwick's forefathers who killed the last of the wolves up here? He has a painting of himself standing with one foot upon the unfortunate creature with a crossbow in his hand. Needless to say, the size of the animal is greatly exaggerated. I am astonished that you have not yet visited the place. Built according to plans by Woodruff and quite magnificent. I shall inform Oliver of your drudgery here and make sure you are invited. I would lose my mind for want of good company and stimulating conversation.'

The Inquisitor stopped himself from denying that his situation in the village was as bleak as he suggested. He had never heard of Woodruff.

'Shall we walk?' Colley looped free his rein and the horse followed obediently behind them.

'What is the purpose of your visit here?' The Inquisitor asked the question before it was asked of him.

'Pleasure, purely. If such a thing exists. I went to visit the abbey on the clifftop. Hilda's monastery. Did you know that the place was once the haunt of countless snakes and that she turned each and every one of them to stone? Here.' He took a black pebble from his pocket and gave it to the Inquisitor to examine. It had been split in half to reveal its spiralling innards.

'And is this a snake turned to stone?'

'If that is what you want it to be.'

'How else would you explain it?'

'I cannot say.'

It occurred to the Inquisitor that he was in the company of a man of great learning, a man whose understanding of the art and the nature of the world around them far outreached his own.

'Keep it. I have others.'

'And what do I say when people ask me what it is?'

'The wisest course would be to tell them that which they wish to hear.'

'Are you a historian?'

'I take some pride in my researches in the subject.'

'Then tell me – did beasts far stranger than any we might see now once roam these moors?'

'I believe that to be true,' Colley said, but elaborated no further.

They walked on in silence for a while.

Then the Inquisitor said, 'I am here because a woman was burned as a witch and her house destroyed with her.' He felt stupid at having expressed himself so clumsily and bluntly, and with such unwarranted determination.

'I know,' Colley said. 'I heard the story from Sir Oliver. If I hadn't met you today I would have paid you a visit once I was settled with him. Do you have a horse?'

'No.'

'A pity. We might have ridden back to the broken cross and searched for its top.'

'And the witch?'

'No woman was ever burned as a witch in this country. Nor ever will be. We are not the heathen Scottish. Nor, I believe, were they so unjustly or severely treated as elsewhere in the country once the charge of witchcraft had been accepted. Certainly, the Church had no hand in the persecutions here-

95

abouts.' He spoke as though he might have had some experience of the matter, but again his tone suggested that he did not wish to pursue the subject.

They parted at the edge of the moor looking down into the village, and mounting his horse John Colley rode away to the north. Neither his path nor his destination were visible, and because they could not be seen so might their existence be denied.

The Inquisitor took out the stone serpent and studied it again as he descended.

17

'We had neither chirurgeons nor nurse-keepers. An apothecary twenty miles distant who sold to us the same worthless cures as all the quacks who rode in advance of the plague and put the fear of God into us with their tales of its approach and its ravages elsewhere, all the better to sell us their own useless, fraudulent remedies.'

Samuel Mercer returned to the room having seen out his housekeeper.

'But the sickness never came,' the Inquisitor said. 'That, surely, is the point.' He noted the magistrate's vague, diverted manner, and though he still felt some sympathy for the tightly sealed vessel of remorse he believed him to have become, he was growing tired of these peripheral diversions, of these arguments and reminiscences which led them away from their main path and into the wastes of other poorly remembered events. He was fighting both the sieve and shield of recollection and his every assault was repulsed.

Samuel Mercer sat beside him. 'It is *your* point. You are a man equipped for the new age which will dawn upon us with the millennium, your life will be lived within it. I, on the other hand, have lived my life, and the only thing I can say with any certainty of this new age is that I shall die within it.'

'Too much is made of marks upon the calendar.'

'Perhaps. But men know what they know, feel what they feel.'

Had the words been spoken by anyone else, the Inquisitor would have dismissed them with a wave. But with Samuel Mercer he waited.

'You see us here. We have no industry to speak of, the land is poor, the roads bad, and yet by some unknown grace we have persisted.'

'And you fear an age that might force change upon you, whether for good or evil?'

'Perhaps.' Samuel Mercer sighed, and the Inquisitor guessed he had missed the point the magistrate was trying to make. He steered them back on to their true course, the one he alone saw ahead through the shadows of the room.

'You speak of the plague,' Samuel Mercer said. 'I sometimes wonder if the alarms and warnings of its supposed approach were not in their own way just as harmful. They bred such a fear so that even to hear a healthy man cough or sneeze you might mark him down as infected and avoid him as though the marks were already blossoming upon him.'

'But the evidence of your own eyes would tell you differently.'

'Evidence! What was that against our souls, our hearts, our minds? Useless adjuncts to the engines which drive us, and in which both our loves and fears reside. In which God himself dwells within us.'

The Inquisitor had arrived an hour earlier, but until the departure of his housekeeper, Samuel Mercer had been unwilling to speak openly, content merely to repeat and have confirmed or denied the gossip of the other villagers, bound by the same tightening threads which encircled them all. He lit a candelabra. The candles were little more than stumps, and dripped their waxy crop all around them. They guttered in the draughts, and as the evening progressed were one by one extinguished, adding to the impression of deepening gloom.

'You know I found the well,' the Inquisitor said.

'And that it is not yet excavated. To what end? No one will return to live there.'

'Perhaps not.'

'Then why?' He was seldom so vigorous in his questioning and this put the Inquisitor on his guard.

'To satisfy myself. Perhaps if the ruins of the house had still been standing then I would have been content to pick through them, perhaps sketch them, and then report that the dwelling was beyond all repair or retrieval.'

'I can see that you are set upon your course.'

'All the more firmly since my every request for assistance has been met with refusal.'

'You should have come here twenty-five years ago. I would have helped you myself.'

'But not now.'

'I am old, weak. Please, do not make me confess any more directly to what I have become. You see me, you know.'

The Inquisitor lowered his head in acknowledgement and apology. Again he was being turned.

'Why will you not tell me what truly happened? Why am I being made to rake through so many ashes, so much dust and powder of evasion and conjecture, to discover for myself what everyone else here already confesses to know?'

'Because confessing to know is not knowing. Because hearing from someone who heard from someone else is not hearing. And perhaps even then – perhaps the agency of hearing or that of sight is in some manner acted upon by heart and mind to provide some comfort so that a man might go on living with himself, in the eyes of the Lord, knowing what he knows, seeing what he has seen, hearing what he has heard.'

'Excuses, all excuses!'

'Excuses for myself. I confess it.'

'No – for all of you. You are right – it *is* a sickness as deadly and all consuming as the plague itself.'

'If that is what you believe then I will not try and convince you otherwise. I cannot agree with you, but then I know only too well how important these false courses are, how necessary our self-deceptions.'

Exasperated, the Inquisitor looked beyond the man, and saw in a sudden flaring of one of the flames the sampler of embroidered names above the mantel, and he understood immediately what Samuel Mercer was saying to him.

'Your wife and daughters. Forgive me. I—'

'No need.'

'Tell me about them.'

'What is there to tell that will make any sense to you, except perhaps for you to know of how they died? Believe me, I am no phoenix risen from these ashes through which you sift.'

It was not what the Inquisitor had intended, but Samuel Mercer went on.

'Their deaths were axe blows to the trunk of a young and vigorous tree. It was not the pestilence you seem so keen upon, but a small pox. The eldest, whose name was Elizabeth after her mother, was taken first. She suffered for almost a month, and for the last week became so thin and debilitated, and was racked with such a burning fever, that she dislocated both her arms in her thrashing about upon the bed. Next died the youngest, Sarah Anne, fourteen months old and still a baby. The Lord was more merciful with her. She was burned and paralysed with the fever, and could neither eat nor drink, and she died in a pool of her own sweat and other liquids only five days after falling ill.'

The Inquisitor was unprepared for this and wanted to stop

him, but saw that this was impossible: the punishing litany must continue; any interruption would be both resented and ignored.

'And last died Mary, the middle one. She was seven years old. Seven years and two days. And if a father can admit to such a thing, she was my favourite. Always ready to sit and read with me, or accompany me on my walks. She loved the hills above us and we lost whole days of our lives together up there. She contracted the fever, but complained little, and in truth it seemed to burn less fiercely inside her, so that our hopes were raised that the Lord might save her. We reasoned that he had punished us enough and that he would now be reconciled to us in a spirit of charity. My wife was already pregnant with our son at that time and I feared for her too, but she continued healthy up until the time of his birth. Mary, my seven-year-old Mary, went blind. The pox erupted more forcibly upon her and ravaged her with a ferocity and a purpose we had not before seen on our other poor daughters. It blinded her and choked her and deafened her. It tore at her through the day and through the night, and she screamed aloud with the unbearable agony of it all. She bled and wept from every orifice. Imagine that if you can, Inquisitor. Imagine that, and imagine too the father to all these sweet and innocent children watching it happen to them and helpless to do anything for them; helpless because he did not know of a cure; helpless because he had been forsaken by the Lord; helpless too because he wished himself dead in their place and could not die. And then even when these three dear innocents were dead and taken away, imagine then this same useless forsaken man visited by the disease himself, imagine him hysterical in his relief that he too was going to join them in the sweet hereafter, in the heaven he had so fervently created in their young unformed minds even as they prepared themselves for entry into it. And then imagine his sorrow that he was to leave behind his beloved wife and unborn child.' He paused, breathless, gulping in air as though he were a swimmer emerged from the sea. And when he spoke again it was with a cold and measured calmness. 'And imagine that same man, a month later, fully recovered, not even pitted by the pox where anyone might see it. Imagine him and his wife clinging to the one ray of light and hope that was their unborn child. Imagine the fears and expectations invested in that unborn child. And when nothing worse could be imagined, see that same man nursing his eight-month-pregnant wife when the pox came and touched her too before mercifully withdrawing and leaving her alive. Axe blows, every one, and afterwards both man and woman unable to stand upright for fear of exposing themselves once again to the blade and being felled for good. But stand they must, and did, even if never fully upright, stand and hear the swish of it returning to them from a great distance, both of them hoping that the other might be spared, and yet both of them clinging to the other like those two trembling trees grown together so that they might either better withstand the blow when it came or so that they might both be finished off by it because the world was no longer a place where one might now live without the other. Imagine that, Inquisitor, and imagine the blade swinging unstoppably towards them out of the darkness, and the woman pulling herself free and throwing herself in its path to stop it and to keep her husband safe. Imagine that, Inquisitor. Imagine all that, and then pray as fiercely and as devoutly as you know how to any god you acknowledge and plead with Him, plead and crave and beg naked and prostrated before Him, that you might be spared a similar display of His mercy, His glory, and His redemption. But make sure your begging is loud, Inquisitor, cup your hands to your mouth and stand upon a high hill, because He may be as deaf to your entreaties as He once was to mine.'

With this the magistrate covered his eyes and wept. His wound was open and, unstanched, his blood flowed.

Still there was nothing the Inquisitor could say.

'Leave me,' Samuel Mercer said eventually. 'But do not feel yourself responsible. I spend many evenings like this; many, but too few. And please, spare me your apologies and regrets. If you had three young daughters and a wife of your own to lose then I might listen to you, but without them you have nothing to say to me. Nothing that might salve your own conscience, and nothing that I might wish to hear.'

The Inquisitor rose and left, and it was only as he stood outside and pulled on his coat that he found himself unable to control the shaking of his hands.

18

He returned to the well. He went alone, and this time took with him an iron stave and a pick to resume his excavation. These were loaned to him by the stonemason, who arrived with them shortly before his departure. He tried to persuade the man to accompany him, knowing how little he would achieve alone, and he sensed a hesitancy in him, as though he were willing to help, but dare not while they were watched and overheard by others in the village. In defiance of these – as many men now as there had once been only women and children – the mason made a show of handing over the tools, a small ceremony almost, and spoke loudly enough for those around them to know what he was doing.

He walked with the Inquisitor to the edge of the woodland, but there he drew back, saying that he would not leave his daughter alone. She had not gone out to work that day and stayed in her bed, and he was fearful for her health in her weakened condition. He barely whispered the words, and the Inquisitor wondered if the girl was not now nurturing something more inside her than her grief.

Before turning away the mason said a strange thing, something he could bring himself to say only at the very point of separation.

He said, 'There are those of us here who secretly support you in what you do. Some of us are not so bound by dark passions and inflammable incredulities as others, and some of us have come every day to regret what happened here, whether living or yet to be born.' He was striding away before the Inquisitor could ask him to elaborate, or who these others were, and he entered the woodland in deep contemplation of what had just been suggested to him.

Arriving at the clearing he saw that the undergrowth he had stacked over the rim of the well to conceal it had been pulled aside, and he approached it with caution, his surprise turning to uncertainty, and then to anger as he realized that someone from the village had come deliberately to obstruct him.

A movement within the trees caught his eye and he called out for whoever was hiding there to reveal themselves.

John Colley appeared, grinning, and with his hands raised in surrender.

The Inquisitor lowered the stave.

'I came from Kepwick hoping to find you here,' Colley said. 'If I'd known you worked alone I would have come dressed and ready to help you. I see you have discovered your well. Is the find of any significance?'

The two men converged on the brick ring.

'Not in itself,' the Inquisitor said. 'But perhaps in the fears and suspicions it seems to evoke in the minds of others.'

'I was talking to my host on the matter. Apparently there is some dispute over the ownership of the woodland at this point.'

'It belongs to the Church,' the Inquisitor said immediately. 'As does – did – this dwelling. That is my whole purpose for being here.'

'I have no argument with you.' Colley crouched down to inspect the circle of bricks. 'It appears soundly constructed. Surprising, wouldn't you say? I doubt if even the wells on the estate are so well steened. What do you intend to prove by clearing it of its rubble? Do you imagine, perhaps, that it is the grave of your witch?'

'Feel free to add your voice to the chorus of mockery.'

The two men laughed.

The notion had occurred to the Inquisitor, but he had dismissed it.

'Lord Kepwick, Oliver, denies that she ever was such a thing. There is no record of any trial, no affidavits or other charges against the poor woman.'

'I knew that long ago.'

'And yet the villagers became her accusers, her judges and executioners.'

'The Commissioners told me – I might say warned me – to ignore what might or might not have happened and to devote my energies solely to an assessment of the site.' It occurred to him as he spoke that the ownership of the land might again be about to be contested in the courts, and that he was there to provide his masters with the report which might strengthen their case as claimants.

John Colley, too, had considered this, and the understanding remained unspoken between them.

'Kepwick did not return here from the Low Countries until long after the woman was killed. He inherited the estate from his uncle, who died fifteen months earlier.'

'Of the plague?'

'What a strange notion. No, he was thrown from his horse and struck his head upon a rock. He survived in a deep sleep for several days and then died. He was unmarried, and Oliver's father, himself killed a decade earlier, was his only brother.'

After this they worked for several hours and excavated the well to a depth of five feet. They took out soil, more broken bricks, and then lengths of charred timber, which Colley arranged on the ground in an effort to see if the pieces fitted together in any way. A broken pot was found, and a triangle of glass, and these too he carefully cleaned and laid out as though they were of some vital significance in reconstructing the whole.

A leather strap appeared at the sunken surface upon which they worked, but was trapped by something beneath and could not be pulled free.

The soil which filled every space around the larger pieces of debris grew moist, and water began to seep up into the hollows from which they drew out the timbers and bricks.

The lining of the well remained largely intact, only here and there missing a piece where either the mortar had rotted and crumbled or a brick had been dislodged by something cast down at the time of the well's destruction.

They worked one man at a time in the enclosed space, and when the emptied cylinder became too deep they withdrew.

'We must pray for a dry night,' Colley said. 'The land is so poorly drained that any rain will fill it to the brim.' He wiped the mud from his arms and legs.

They parted, having agreed to meet again in two days' time.

Colley was hunting on the moor the next day with his host, and the Inquisitor declined his offer to accompany them.

Emerging back among the village fields, he saw another of the fires which burned across the stubble, tended by the men in the same casual manner they herded their recalcitrant cattle and swine in and out of the village each day. The cream and yellow ground turned to black, only here and there retaining its original colour where the flames parted or missed and left behind them islands of Saint Luke's summer amid the darkening tide.

19

'*You* dare to question *me* about the nature of our evidence, about the integrity of our witnesses?' Jonas Webster had been striding away across the hillside, but stopped himself, as though at the command of some irresistible inner compulsion, and turned back to confront the Inquisitor, who stood above the ellipse of halo already outlined in the chalk. 'By what right? Upon whose authority? Your masters'? Your masters who bestir themselves oh so rarely and reluctantly to find out for themselves how the Lord is obeyed and his work carried out in these distant and forgotten realms? These men? They are money-lenders in His house and I shall never, never hold myself responsible to them.'

The Inquisitor, though prepared, was taken aback by the violence of this outburst. He was also strangely reassured by it. He had put his question directly upon meeting the man because here too he was tired of the game of diversion and allusion, whose rules of engagement he little understood.

Jonas Webster came quickly back to him, not caring whether he walked on the turf or the clean rock. He stopped with his face only a few inches from the Inquisitor's, his pointing finger almost touching his chest, ready to jab.

'The witnesses of centuries,' he said, his voice a rasp, a self-congratulatory and malicious whisper. 'The *Summis Desi-*

derantes Affectibus, the *Malleus Maleficarum*, the *Formicarius*.' He recited the titles as though each were a blow that might knock a man senseless.

The Inquisitor was familiar with them all. 'All discredited,' he said.

'Never! What a harvest of evil and malefaction they gathered in, what pyres and passages and cleansing blazes they filled and lighted.' Jonas Webster threw up his hands in a sudden fire. 'If you wish to talk to me of discredited men, then talk to me of Hopkins, of the damner damned. Talk to me of the look in his eyes when *he* floated and was condemned. Imagine, if you must, *his* passage into the furnace, tormented to the end of time by those for whom his own tormenting might have lasted only minutes.' He spoke with relish. Spittle formed in bubbles on his lips. 'Imagine him passed from hand to hand, each a claw to squeeze him and scratch him and pull from him an ounce of his own worthless flesh until he too was so completely destroyed that—' He stopped abruptly and wiped his mouth.

'I am no Hopkins. That is not my purpose here.'

'Even if it were, you come too late for any of that. But, oh how times change, Inquisitor. Tell me – how are we to change with them?'

'Perhaps we might change by purging ourselves, by seeking more assiduously after the truth of our own history.'

'And deny all recriminations? Riddles, wasted intellect and energy.'

'Then instead of Hopkins, imagine the woman judged innocent in the eyes of the Lord and saved from Hell. Imagine her at the gates of Heaven waiting beside the keepers there to point out to them her own persecutors, and by so doing damning *them* to everlasting—'

109

'Impossible! Speculation. She was damned by her own actions, by the freaks and misfortunes she visited on all those around her.'

'Of which nothing can be proven.'

'*Haeresis est maxima opera maleficarum non credere.*'

To disbelieve in witchcraft is the greatest of heresies.

'A convenient epigraph for the *Malleus*, don't you think?'

'And not one that will be scorned by you.' His finger came back close to the Inquisitor's chest. 'The *Daemonolatreia*—'

'Repeated that man, by the acquisition of some unspecified arcane knowledge, might make the angels work for him and thus control the movements of Heaven.'

Jonas Webster was silenced.

'And by an extension of such logic, it was perhaps not unreasonable for ordinary men to suppose that witches, by a baser acquisition of power, might make devils work for them and thus interfere with events here on earth.'

'You twist and confuse the words of men more qualified than yourself,' Jonas Webster said.

'No. I merely repeat them. Their logic was perverse in the first instance.'

'And so the angels—'

'Were divided, and half of them possessed by the Devil and harnessed to his own ends.'

'And you seek to deny him by refuting all evidence of the men who have experience of him and his works?'

'No, I seek only to discover for myself how this one poor woman was condemned and killed.'

'She condemned herself,' Jonas Webster said, and again he took several paces away before returning.

It was midday. They were alone on the hillside, and the angel beneath them, hidden from them by the curve of the land, was nearing completion.

The Inquisitor guessed that the parson was close to telling him something of significance.

'A creature, a fox or stray dog, was one night discovered digging at our laystalls, digging to expose and then devour the excrement buried there, and a man came upon it and fired his sling at it, hitting it on the leg and causing it to yelp with pain and limp away as best it could. Two days later the woman entered the village with a limp herself, and a month after that the man who had fired his sling was dead of some unknown cause. I myself kicked a screaming cat that would not let me sleep, and which I caught by surprise before it could spring away.'

'And a short while afterwards the woman—'

'Appeared with a bruise on her cheek.'

Was there nothing he had not heard before? 'And her explanation?'

'That she had fallen.'

'And no one believed her?'

'*I* did not believe her.'

'And what you believed, so others believed.'

Jonas Webster only stared at him.'

'Tell me, did you persecute her for long? Did you torture her? Did she confess?'

'She did not need to confess. Her actions alone betrayed her.'

The Inquisitor fought to control his anger at the man. His fists formed so tightly that his nails dug into his palms.

'He was incubus to her, and she was succubus to another.'

'The Dutchman.'

'Both of them acting at the Antichrist's behest to recover his lost kingdom.' Jonas Webster's eyes gleamed as he spoke.

'None of which was ever proven in a court of law.'

'Perhaps not. But I doubt if even you, Inquisitor, have the

111

courage of your convictions to see that the omission, worthless as it might be, is remedied now. As I say, you are no longer servant to the cleansers, but to the moneylenders.'

The Inquisitor considered his answer. 'Decent, honest men live and die by their decency and honesty.' It was something his father had once written to another, and something he secretly hoped might one day be inscribed upon his own gravestone.

'Search the woods around where she lived,' Jonas Webster said, believing he had exposed some flaw or weakness in the other. 'See how well the monkshood and the vervain and the hellebore grow.'

'Protection against insanity of the mind, not the insanity of the age,' the Inquisitor said quietly, and he too retreated beyond the reach of provocation.

20

The next day he woke before dawn. He believed he had cried out in his sleep and woken himself. He was sitting upright with his arms before him as though to push someone away or to protect himself from something. He looked at them for a moment, confused, and unable to distinguish between what he saw and felt upon waking and what in his dream still caused him to tremble and hold out his arms. His teeth chattered and he sweated heavily.

Outside it was raining, and the water blew in squalls against the small window.

He heard voices in the darkness and then found that he was talking to himself. He asked himself why he had come to this place, why he had truly come, what he hoped to achieve there, and when, if ever, he intended to leave. He looked into the empty hearth and saw there a roaring blaze. But then he looked into the flames and saw only the cold grate on which there appeared sudden circles where the rain fell down the chimney and landed like black pearls on the stone.

He slept again, or knew he must have done, because when he next looked at the window it was a square of bronze light, catching the rising sun, focusing and turning its strengthening glare until its rays were directed upon him where he lay, simultaneously blinding and chilling him. He stopped himself from crying out. His hands still shook and he still sweated heavily. His face was slick with wet and his hair hung over his eyes. He licked his dry lips and tasted salt on them.

An hour later he woke again and the sun was gone. He heard voices beneath him and footsteps on the landing outside his room. He called out, or believed he called out, for like a drunken man he could not remember having said the words the moment they were spoken. He shouted for whoever was outside to come in, but no one entered. For an instant he believed there was already someone else there in the room with him, and for less than the time it took him to blink and make this other figure disappear, he believed it to have been his own father – not his father as he had known him only as a young child, but his father as he had become, subject to the ravages of his mortal wounds and the weight of the earth which pressed down on him in his grave. It was too much for him, and as he closed his eyes he cried out again, half calling for the figure to be gone, and half screaming as though to shake this apparition into some awareness of him so that it might vanish of its own accord. Beneath him the voices ceased; outside all was silent.

When he woke for a third time it was with the shock of a prodded dreamer.

Two men stood above the bed and looked down at him. He recognized neither of them, although they spoke to him in low and reassuring voices, which even in this new delirium suggested to him some degree of acquaintance.

An instant later he was alone, sitting upright and breathing deeply and looking into the coals of the fire which now burned in the grate. He felt light-headed, and his every movement, however slight, made him giddy. Beside him lay a bowl of liquid and a plate of food. He put his hands together and said a prayer, interrupted before it was half finished by a knock on the door.

Samuel Mercer came in, cautiously, as though in anticipation of disturbing him.

'They sent for me,' he said, again cautiously, as though the words were intended to explain a great deal more which must remain unspoken.

'Am I ill?' the Inquisitor asked him, allowing himself to enter into the conspiracy of uncertain comforts and necessary deceits which exist between the nurse and the nursed.

'You were brought back here by Jonas Webster and the mason.'

'What do you mean "brought back here"? I have been here all night.'

The magistrate pretended to busy himself at the fire.

A sudden fear stabbed at the Inquisitor. He felt it moving deep inside him, as though it were a live thing, an eel perhaps, muscular and uncontained, which he had swallowed.

'You were found on the moor,' Samuel Mercer said, sufficiently encouraged by the words to return to the bed. 'The mason's daughter has taken to walking in the night. Her father has known about this for some time but told no one. She returned to him last night in a panic saying she had seen ... saying she had seen you and that you were acting strangely, wildly. He set out alone to bring you back and encountered Jonas Webster on his way to find you. The parson insisted on going with him.'

'But how can I have been out? I swear to you I never left this room. Where are my wet clothes?' The words fought hard against the disbelief which framed them.

'It has been a fine night.'

'It rained!'

'Perhaps a dream ... your fever.'

The Inquisitor looked to where he had seen the sooty droplets spend themselves in the hearth. There was nothing there.

'I wore no clothes?' the Inquisitor said.

115

'It is of no matter. You are ill.'

'But the girl. I . . .'

'She is young. Her mind remains unbalanced. I believe it is best for everyone if nothing is said.'

The Inquisitor started to shake and Samuel Mercer pulled up his blankets and pinned them across his chest, as much to restrain as to warm him.

'I have to see her, to see her father, to explain.'

'He wishes no one to see her.'

'Then let me send word.' His teeth were again chattering. 'I'll explain everything to him.'

'Oh, God, what did she think she had encountered?'

'Rest.'

'It wasn't me. It can't have been. I was never out of this room. Why would she lie about such a thing? It must have been someone else she saw. Jonas Webster has poisoned her mind. Tell him I want to see him. I want to hear the words from his own lips that it was me he saw up there.'

Samuel Mercer shook his head. 'Impossible, I'm afraid. He is away on Church business for a few days.'

The Inquisitor laughed. 'And left already, I suppose.' He was growing weaker.

'Why not? It is late afternoon.'

'Impossible. The morning – I—'

Samuel Mercer stood back from him. 'Your confusion is entirely natural.'

'I am not confused,' the Inquisitor shouted, but the words dried up in his throat along with his conviction.

He lay back and closed his eyes. He heard the magistrate leave the room, heard him speak to someone who had been waiting outside.

He resumed his interrupted prayer, but was asleep with his hands clasped upon his chest before it was finished.

116

21

When next he woke he was sufficiently recovered to remember everything that had passed between himself and Samuel Mercer, and to distinguish between that which had truly happened and those less welcome memories of his feverish nightmares. But he still had no recollection of being on the moor, or of encountering the girl and being brought down by her father and Jonas Webster. He could not decide which concerned him the most – the fact of his forgotten nocturnal wanderings, his encounter with the girl, or the knowledge that Jonas Webster had played some intimate part in these unaccountable events.

He felt weak with a ravenous hunger and saw that the bowl and plate had been taken from beside him. He tried to stand up but barely possessed the strength to swing his legs from the bed. Instead he pulled straight his blankets and called for someone to attend to him.

The sun still shone, and noticing the reflected pane of quivering light on the ceiling above him, his attention was drawn to the small bundle of leaves and stems hanging in the window. Whether these had been left because they were believed to possess medicinal powers or whether they were hung simply as some token or charm, he could not tell; he suspected the latter. He had seen them elsewhere in the village; they were to the houses what the crucified crows were to the planted fields.

A woman whom he recognized, but to whom he had never before spoken, entered. She brought him soup and warm water. She seemed surprised to see him sitting upright in bed, and remained silent. He nodded at her, knowing that she did not wish the silence to be broken. She paused before leaving and turned back to look at him. She drew a breath, as though about to speak, but said nothing; she went instead to a drawer and took from it a looking glass. She held this to her chest with both hands, undecided about what she intended to do. And then she laid it face down on the bed and left him before he could respond to her strange actions.

He dipped a cloth into the warm water and held it over his eyes. His tongue felt leaden and dry in his mouth, and his lips were cracked. He saw on the forefinger of his right hand a whitlow, newly formed. He prodded it and winced at the pain. Elsewhere his hands were unwashed and scratched, and dirt lay beneath every nail. He remembered having scrubbed them upon his return from the well. The whitlow would need to be cut open and allowed to drain. He looked at it as the pain subsided, looked at it as though it was undeniable proof of all the magistrate had suggested to him, looked at it as though it was some judgement upon him.

He picked up the bowl of soup, held it to his mouth, but could not bring himself to drink from it. Balls of yellow fat floated on its surface, and the bread over which it had been poured had disintegrated and looked now like sodden mould. He felt as though he was going to be sick and he set the bowl back down until he felt recovered.

Then he leaned slowly forward, retrieved the looking glass, and looked into the face which had so alarmed the woman. Four days' growth of beard covered his chin and cheeks. There was no colour to his skin, only the dark mask of sickness round his eyes. He opened his mouth and saw that his teeth too were discoloured, and that they were separated by dark lines. He licked at them and felt a fine grit on his tongue.

As he tried to account for this there was a knock at the door, and before he could put down the glass and make himself more presentable, Jonas Webster came in, stood by the window and looked at him intently.

'I owe you my thanks,' the Inquisitor said.

'I do my duty to man and God. It is the girl to whom I devote my attention now.' He spun the bundle of leaves as he spoke.

'Is she suffering?'

'Her mind is invaded. Her father has restrained her and watches over her day and night.'

'I will visit him to thank him personally.'

'He will not see you. He will see no one.'

It seemed the animosity between the two men could not now be contained and the veneer of cold civility was rubbed ever thinner with everything that passed between them.

'Samuel Mercer tells me I was found on the moor. I must have collapsed.' It was an inadequate attempt to draw Jonas Webster out, and the man retained his advantage.

'Perhaps you work too hard at the house. You are a man of letters, a cultivated man, not a labourer.'

'You've been there?' the Inquisitor said.

'I have.'

'With your angel-makers?'

'Ah, my brute myrmidons. To see what it was that obsesses you so.'

'You knew that already.'

'I hunted with Kepwick three days ago. A standing invitation, but not one he extends with any true grace. I met your historian friend. Rest assured that no one has tampered with your work during your absence. He has seen to that.'

119

'And your business away. I expected you to be gone for some time yet.'

'My business is my affair. And I stay away no longer than is necessary. But if you must know, I am negotiating with the Bishop to block up our leper hole.'

'I didn't realize the church possessed one.'

'The judicious cultivation of one of our yews.' He almost laughed at the cleverness of the remark.

He left several minutes later, saying that he was going to kneel in prayer for an hour in the stoneyard.

22

Two days later he was well enough to leave his room and walk the short distance to Samuel Mercer's house.

Immediately he entered, the magistrate held out a letter to him. The Inquisitor read it. It was a brief note from his wife's parents informing him that their grandson, the magistrate's son, would be coming to stay with his father for a week, and that he would be arriving in ten days' time on the thirty-first of October.

The formality of the communication surprised the Inquisitor and he did not know how to respond.

'You must look forward to seeing him,' he said, waiting for something from the other so that he might better gauge his feelings on the matter.

'He comes every year.'

'Does he not write himself?'

'Never. They make all the arrangements on his behalf. They employ their own coachman so that he might come to me directly from them.'

'Will they not come with him?'

'They will never come here as long as they live.'

'Will they not even come to see you?'

'I exist only because my son exists. I killed their daughter and their three other grandchildren, remember.' He took back the sheet of paper, folded it and slid it into the book by his side. Then he took the book and hid it among a thousand others on

121

his shelves. The Inquisitor looked around him and imagined thirty other volatile charges, hidden, their precise whereabouts unknown, but all of them ready to detonate an explosion in even the most careless of hearts at the unsuspecting turn of a page. He remained silent, not wishing to prolong the man's suffering. The visits were occasions of filial duty, cold fires, worthless gems.

'It is good to see you recovered,' Samuel Mercer said. He paused on his way back to his seat and looked at the shelves around him.

But the Inquisitor was not recovered. He had no appetite and his nights were still largely sleepless, and his sleep tormented.

'You would be wise to gain sufficient more of your lost strength and then leave. Winter is a hard time here. Snow blossoms on the moor and then spills over us like a pillow fallen from a bed. The river freezes along even its more turbulent reaches and the air grows so cold that we pad our mouths with cloths before venturing out. Men have seen smoke from the chimneys freeze in the air and fall all around them like pumice. And for those of us grown old here our hearts are not the warming furnaces they once were.'

'Then would it not be a better plan for your son to visit you in the spring or summer?'

'I have no say in the matter. I believe his guardians have a regular arrangement to visit some other ageing relatives else-where and he comes to me when they themselves depart.'

'What is his work?'

'He does not work. They make no demands on him and provide him with everything he needs. Please, it is a personal matter, and I would rather not speak of it. I believe the hunting on the moors has gone well this year.'

The path divided and then the two new paths divided.

'Several score of woodcock and snipe. Mostly netted.' The Inquisitor had learned this from his landlord.

For the next hour their conversation was desultory, each man bound up in his own thoughts.

'I wish you to show me something,' the Inquisitor said as he prepared to leave.

'If it is within my power.'

The two men walked to the churchyard and the magistrate pointed out the sculpted yew bush which grew close to the wall, behind which the leper hole gave a view into the body of the church.

'Were there ever many?' the Inquisitor asked him.

'I doubt it. But the moor was said to attract them by its isolation and emptiness. They were said to gather up there.'

'And then come down here and kneel in prayer at this hole whenever a service was conducted.'

'Once a month. By arrangement. Everyone else would be in church and those poor unfortunates who still insisted upon some form of spiritual succour came down unseen, usually only one or two at a time, so that they might at least convince themselves that they had in some way participated and received some blessing or benediction.'

The Inquisitor tried to bend the bush aside, but it grew stubbornly over the hole. He could see only the sill and the ungiving hassock, both worn smooth with the weight of devotion. He tried to imagine the deformed, peering faces, listening to the sermons, hymns, and prayers within, and seeing only the backs of the congregation turned resolutely against them.

'Come away,' the magistrate told him. He complied, and the sentinel bush sprang immediately back to take its place at the holy ramparts.

23

A further five days passed before he was sufficiently recovered to return to the well, and discover there its terrible secret.

He had been visited twice during his convalescence by John Colley with tales of the hunt, and was reassured by him that there had been no disturbance at the site of the house.

In common with others who saw him, Colley was alarmed by the Inquisitor's changed appearance. He was due to leave Kepwick and return home in two days' time, and the Inquisitor sensed that he had lost interest in the excavation, that he had hoped to gain more from their companionship. Neither man confronted the other with his beliefs.

They met in the woodland. On this occasion they had with them ropes and pails and were able to clear away more quickly the saturated debris which filled the well.

More of the leather strap was revealed, and now when the Inquisitor pulled on it he felt it give slightly beneath him. He had convinced himself that it was the strap by which the woman had been bound, and that it, and more – perhaps even the instruments of her torture – had been thrown down the well and then the well demolished to hide these for ever.

'It snags on something,' he called out.

Colley showed less concern, but he took his place at the bottom of the well and continued to clear away the rubble and dig deeper into its secrets, working up to his knees in a broth of risen water.

The Inquisitor lay on the flattened mound of the house. He was not as fully recovered as he tried to convince himself, and was quickly exhausted by his labours, and while Colley dug out and threw up the waste he cleaned and sorted it into separate piles.

'Give me a hand,' Colley then shouted, only his head visible above the hole in which he stood. He had fastened a rope to the strap and he passed this up to the Inquisitor so that they might both pull on it.

It came slowly. A disturbance in the sediment turned the water black and the surface looked as though it was beginning to boil. At first there was little give in the rope and the strap, but the something beneath shifted and it came more easily.

'It's free,' Colley called up, and when finally there was no further resistance to their efforts they stopped pulling.

They rested for a moment, and then Colley cried out and thrust his hands beneath the water. He called again, first, 'No!' and then, 'Help me,' and then he slipped beneath the surface as he lost his footing, rising gasping, his hair matted and his face brown with the mud in which he had been immersed. He tried to scramble up the sheer sides and the Inquisitor lay flat on the ground and reached down to help him. Their hands clasped and then their grip was lost. The Inquisitor swung the rope around his waist and told Colley to grab hold of it, still uncertain of what had alarmed the man other than his loss of footing. Finally, Colley was able to pull himself free. He lay panting on the grass, wiping the slime from his eyes and mouth.

'I lost my balance; something moved beneath me.'

'We disturbed the sediment.'

'No, something more. Something attached to the strap.

125

We pulled something up and it floated free. I felt it rise against my legs.'

'A rotted timber perhaps.' He dare not say what he believed they had discovered.

John Colley shook his head.

The Inquisitor crawled back to the hole and saw the leather strap stretched taut between the surface of the water and the rim. He picked up the rope to which it was still attached, and, ensuring that he stood far enough back from the crumbling lip of the well, he tugged on it. Again the water boiled and the rope fell slack. He looked down and gasped at what he saw. A dislodged brick fell away beneath him and he stepped back.

'What is it?' Colley asked him, rising to his feet and coming to see for himself.

The Inquisitor pointed.

Colley joined him and looked down.

Beneath them, floating in the water, was a body, the strap attached to its neck. It was recognizable as neither man nor woman, its head flattened and smooth like a deflated bladder, tanned the colour of leather, eyeless, but with its teeth showing and with hair still plastered to its scalp. A beckoning hand broke the surface close by and gestured to them in its new-found buoyancy.

'Is it her?' Colley said.

The Inquisitor could not speak. He stared intently at the distorted features, at the squashed nose and crushed cheeks, and at the silent cry of agony that might have been drawn back upon its lips. The strap was knotted at the back of the neck. And he knew in that instant that it was not the woman, not *his* woman. He could not tell how he knew, only that he knew, and that his every expectation had been confounded.

'It's a man,' he said eventually, and as he spoke so he

126

realized how much he did know and could now say for certain. 'It's the man who came to live with her, the Dutchman.'

'Then God rest his soul,' Colley said. He looked down open-mouthed at the man's head, and at his hand still gently bobbing on the surface, its smooth palm and curled fingers held up to them as though in supplication, nothing to choose between the colour of his skin and the colour of the water in which he had for so long been immersed. They could only guess how terrible his death had been.

They took up the rope together and pulled on it. The body rose higher in the water. An arm revealed itself. Then the collar and sleeve of a jacket, then the jacket itself and another arm. Released from the water, this second limb rose stiffly until it rested above the man's head, as though even now he were trying to protect himself. They looked down upon him as his persecutors must have last seen him. In place of pleading, water dribbled from his nose and mouth, and these unnatural move-ments, perverse duplications, were almost too much for the two men to bear.

Recovering from what they saw, they raised the drowned man until the water no longer supported him, but knew that they dare not risk taking his weight on the strap alone.

John Colley searched out the longest timber they had so far retrieved, and probed with this beneath the water until he felt the man's legs, levering him higher until, with great reluctance, they were able to grab hold of his shoulders and pull him over the rim. They did this quickly, fearful that his sodden flesh might slip from his skeleton into their hands like overcooked meat from its bones.

But he rose intact and was laid down intact, the body fixed more in the semblance of peaceful sleep than in the unendurable pose of its last drawn breath.

They knelt on the ground beside him.

Water dripped from his clothes and limbs. His face shone and then dried, and he looked almost at peace.

'The sleep of the dead,' Colley said, then turned away and began to retch violently on to the grass.

24

Time passed. The clear sky above them filled with cloud, and where they rested on the ground they felt cold after the heat of their exertions. They lay alongside the corpse, their heads close to the man's own. They speculated on how he had died, and the Inquisitor told John Colley what others had already told him. He knew he was repeating lies and speculation nurtured in prejudice, but the very presence of the body so close to them, and brought back into the light of day by their own labours, demanded some explanation, however imperfect.

'Judas,' Colley said absently. 'He too was cast down a well and hauled back out again.'

'Alive?'

John Colley nodded. His eyes were focused on the man's mouth, on his teeth and the root of tongue pressed sideways into his cheek, the rest of the space plugged with mud. 'Some say he – Judas – some say he betrayed Christ merely to hasten his own redemption.'

'This is not he,' the Inquisitor said simply, knowing that, if nothing else, then the man deserved better than to have his own fate so conveniently explained, understood and accepted.

They took the strap from around his neck and searched his pockets. They found nothing, only an empty purse. The strap was loose and had not been used to hang him, merely as a halter by which he had been led. There was a ring on one of his fingers, but the pickled skin had folded around this and neither of them attempted to remove it.

Colley sat with the man's hand in his own, his waning interest revived. The Inquisitor wiped hair from the creased forehead now that it had dried a little, surprised at how easily it responded to his touch. Surprised too at the roughness of the bristles which covered the man's chin, and which he had shaved into a small pointed beard.

The cloud above them thickened and it started to rain, lightly at first, but then more heavily, and then with an intensity which forced them to shelter in the surrounding trees. They stood beneath the largest of these, pressed to its trunk, and tried unsuccessfully to shake the wetness from their clothes. Above them the water gathered and drained from leaves and branches and fell to the earth like spent shot, pitting the ground.

The corpse left behind in the clearing regained the lustre with which it had risen from the well. It was washed clean and turned to copper.

Colley and the Inquisitor watched this. Neither man spoke. It was as though both shared the same ridiculous notion that this cleansing downpour might in some way invigorate the long-dead man, that the liquid, this ichor, might rehydrate his dried muscle and flesh, and that he might stir, yawn, turn his head, push himself upright, and rub his empty eyes as though he were waking confused from some long sleep.

The spell was broken by Colley, who said, 'We cannot leave him there.'

The Inquisitor nodded his agreement. He was shivering and his senses were dulled. An ember of his fever still glowed within him and he knew that he had fanned it into life with his exertions. He tried to hide his trembling limbs from Colley, but Colley saw this, and without speaking he alone left their shelter, returned to the man, and dragged him back to the well. He held him beneath his arms, his head resting slackly on his chest, and positioning his feet above the water, he lowered him until he could bear the weight no longer and then let the man drop. A sheen of brown rose to cover him, and on his way back to the sheltering tree he held up his face and hands to the rain so that he too might be cleansed.

The Inquisitor was sitting when he returned, shaking, his arms held tightly across his chest as though to contain his convulsions.

'I'll walk with you to the village, see you safely back,' Colley told him. He could not disguise the concern in his voice.

'No.' The Inquisitor would listen to none of his entreaties. 'We are being punished.' But the words were mumbled and incomprehensible, and when Colley tried to help him stand he pushed him away and started back along the path alone.

He walked and ran, and all too often stumbled and fell. He shouted back for the man who was no longer behind him to stop following him.

The path was exposed to the rain and so he left it and created a new one beneath the canopy. He struggled to control his senses. He knew that the village lay to his right and that if he continued in that direction then he must eventually emerge from the trees into farmland, and that once out in the open he would be able to orientate himself more accurately.

The ground turned soft beneath his feet and now when he fell he buried his face in the soft earthy deposits of ten autumns past. Exposed roots tripped him. In his blindness he ran into trees, and the branches of those he avoided reached out to lash him.

He did not know how long he had been running, and when exhaustion finally overtook him he knew only that he had turned from his path too many times to any longer be on a direct course for the village.

The rain continued to fall. He lay for several minutes where he collapsed, then as he pushed himself up his arm sank to the shoulder in a pit of mud. In his surprise he called out for help, but was then able to extricate himself. He sweated heavily. One moment his legs felt as though they had turned to lead, and the next as though they were brittle stalks ready to give way beneath him at the slightest effort. He wiped his hands on his jacket, but succeeded only in pressing the wetness through to his undershirt and then his chest and stomach. He found himself tearing at his clothes, as though these hampered him in his flight. He believed he called out continually, but when he stopped to listen for any answer, he heard neither the words nor their echo.

He ran, and then turned and ran in the opposite direction. He dropped to his knees and prayed. He cut his forehead and the blood ran into his eyes and mouth, and when he saw this in his palm he fell fully to the ground, wept aloud for a few seconds, and then passed out.

PART III

PART III

25

When he came round it was no longer raining. He felt his head supported by something soft. His arms lay by his side and when he clutched at the sheets of his bed his hands came up full of leaves and soil.

Someone spoke to him. A man held his face close to his own and supported his head from behind. He looked up into the face and saw that it was black, as though all the skin had been burnt, and that its white showed through only in rings around the man's eyes and within reach of his tongue around his lips.

This man spoke to him, but he could not understand him. The man glanced away and the Inquisitor saw that there were others standing close by. These too were blackened, their flesh and their clothes.

He tried to speak to the man, but could not.

The first coherent thought he was able to form was to wonder whether or not he was still lying where he had fallen – although he did not remember this – or if he had been found by this strange band of men and carried elsewhere by them.

The ground felt unnaturally warm. He saw smoke rising behind the other figures, and then watched as one of them raked at the earth and turned it instantly to fire. Others were attracted by the man's actions and they too prodded the dark ground and turned it to flame.

He felt himself lifted further upright and then felt the hard rim of a cup pressed to his lips. He drank from this, and as his lips parted to receive the liquid so the cup was tipped towards him and his mouth was filled with a hot and bitter concoction. He coughed and spat to clear his throat, and his eyes watered at the taste. The man holding the cup was not alarmed by this, and waiting until he had stopped choking, he lifted the cup again to his lips and indicated for him to drink. This time the Inquisitor sipped more gently and the liquid did not burn him.

'You drink that,' the man holding his head said to him.

He drained the cup and afterwards took several deep breaths and allowed himself to be pulled upright and propped with his back against a fallen trunk. A dirty fleece was wrapped around his shoulders and another draped across his legs.

'He found you,' the man said, indicating one of the others, who paused for a moment in his raking of the burning earth and looked towards the Inquisitor.

The Inquisitor tried to thank him, but before he could form the words the man had turned back to his work.

'He brought you here because you were laid out in the rain. He said your horse had thrown you, but there was no horse.'

'Do you know who I am?'

The man nodded. 'And the work upon which you and your friend have been engaged.'

'You were watching?'

'We work here, and while we are here we live with our work. Others have come into the woods from the fields hoping to see you, but their fear has held them back.'

A call from one of the others caused the man to rise, and he left the Inquisitor where he sat. The men had gathered at a mound of earth, and when they were all arranged in a circle around this they scraped together at its base with their rakes and staves. This time a dozen hidden fires erupted from the ground as though blown out by a single pair of bellows. Sparks erupted high into the dim light and rose like fireflies through the branches. The earth burned even brighter and the mound collapsed amid a rush of gaseous flame.

Only then did it occur to the Inquisitor that he was watching the charcoal burners, and he almost laughed out in his relief.

The man came back to him.

'You are the burners,' the Inquisitor said to him.

The man wiped his face with a cloth dipped in a pail. 'Would you rather have us for murderers and thieves like the rest of them?'

Several of the others came to join him. Those left behind continued to push and rake at the collapsing mound until it was levelled, and until it hissed and smoked upon the wet leaves over which it flowed like lava. Smaller fires sprang up and were stamped out. Individual timbers were seized and pulled aside.

More of the liquid was brought to the Inquisitor, and this time he held the cup himself. He was offered bread but refused it.

'How far am I from the village?'

'A mile. You were running in the wrong direction.'

He wondered how much more the burners had seen.

'Can you help me to get back there?'

The man nodded. 'When you are strong enough.'

'I must get back now.'

The burner considered this and then called for two others to help the Inquisitor to his feet.

He felt he had recovered, sitting on the ground, but as he rose his head spun and his legs would not respond to his commands. His face was again bathed in sweat, which the man wiped with his cloth.

The two burners stood on either side of him, held their arms beneath his own and then joined hands across his back. He stood propped between them and was able to move forward with his feet barely touching the ground.

As they were about to leave, the man who had tended to him picked up one of the fleeces and fastened it again around his shoulders. The Inquisitor promised to return it when he was well.

The man put his mouth close to the Inquisitor's ear, said, 'Leave him where you found him,' and then withdrew before the Inquisitor could respond, turning back to his task of spreading and cooling the glowing timbers.

It was as the Inquisitor considered his reply that his attention was drawn to a clearing beside the men. Several saplings had been stripped of their leaves and branches and then folded together to form a simple arch to which slabs of bark had then been fastened, creating a miniature shelter or alcove. Inside this, standing with his arms and legs outstretched, stood a small child, naked, it seemed, and motionless, and gazing directly out at him.

The sight of this small mute figure shocked him and he felt himself sag between the two men who supported him.

'What is it?' he asked.

Neither man would answer him. Instead they led him towards the shelter until he was close enough to look down at the carving and see the cut-off stumps which served for arms and legs, and the eyes which had been branded with a poker into the otherwise featureless face. He saw too the exaggerated genitalia, bulbous and gnarled with the grain of the wood, hanging midway to the small figure's knees.

'Our shrine,' the man who had tended to him said. And as he spoke he knelt and rearranged the bark walls until the figure was enclosed and hidden from view.

26

He recovered in his bed for three days, and during that time the news of what he and John Colley had found spread to every house in the village; few learned what they did not already know: what was now brought into the light had never been hidden; what was now put into words had never truly been sealed in silence.

For those three days he saw no one but his landlord, and one of the girls employed to tend to his needs. Food and drink were served to him, and coals carried up for his fire, but largely all this was brought to him as he slept – whether out of a desire not to disturb him as he rested or because these servants were fearful of confronting him he did not know.

He expected daily a visit from Jonas Webster or the magistrate, and was disappointed when neither came.

Webster, he guessed, would be preoccupied with the completion of his angel, the work having acquired a new urgency in the ever-spreading shadow of all that had recently happened. And Samuel Mercer, he imagined, would be preparing himself for the imminent arrival of his son.

He woke on one occasion to find part of his hand bandaged, three fingers bound together, and he guessed that his whitlow had either burst or been lanced. The dressing was tight and its knot secure. A small stain showed through the material, neither red nor coloured by pus, and he sniffed at this.

At first he detected nothing, but having cleared his nose he was then repulsed by the faint odour of decay which seeped through.

He could remember little of the previous days or of his journey through the trees supported by the two men. Nor could he remember if they had climbed the stairs with him or left him in the doorway and summoned the landlord. But as he laid his bandaged hand on the bed beside him there returned to him the vivid and unexpected memory of something he had seen upon emerging from the woodland and entering the village beside the communal barn at the edge of the houses. Night had fallen by then, and the men supporting him kept away from every light. As they passed the barn the two burners increased their pace. A stronger light than elsewhere fell from its open door, and the noise of winnowing and the voices and laughter of men and women could be heard inside. He remembered looking into the building as he was hurried past and seeing those gathered there flailing at the grain, seeing it rise and fall around them in a storm of chaff, seeing some of the figures lost in this, and others made indistinct, liquid and ghostlike, by it, and by the dust of powdery light which engulfed them and was reflected all around them. But rather than avoiding this blinding, choking storm, it seemed to the Inquisitor, in the glimpse he was able to catch of this frenzied action so unnaturally illuminated, that these men and women were almost dancing within the cloud, grabbing up handfuls of grain and throwing it above them and all around them, not in the slightest concerned for the powder in their eyes and hair, or for the suffocating dust in their throats.

It was the glimpse of an instant, and in the blink of an eye it was passed, or, rather, he was past it, hurried further into the enveloping darkness by the two men. He could not remember if he had told them to stop or to take him back so that he might confirm what he had seen. They would not have obeyed him,

140

not have lingered. Or had he in truth witnessed none of this? Was he not now deceived in recollection merely of a nightmare, or something half seen and imperfectly understood, something tainted by an overactive imagination still at the height of its own unstoppable fever? But there was something else he remembered, something else he had seen, and recollecting this now as vividly as the remainder of the scene, he felt convinced that in this instance he *had* been witness to what was now so clearly and unshakeably drawn in his mind's eye. He remembered that at the centre of this maelstrom of light and activity and noise there stood a solitary figure, a woman, whose face was smeared with some colour but whom he felt certain he recognized, and who stood alone, immobile, as though detached from the frantic ceremony unfolding all around her, as though stupefied, deaf and blind to it, her face registering nothing of what she must have seen and heard and felt as the flailers circled her and showered her with the powder which reduced them all to watery, fractured outlines, devoid of recognizable substance or form. And he remembered something else too – he remembered she had looked directly out at him, but that in the instant their eyes had met he had been pulled away by the burners and was plunged with them into the darkness, and that, unfixed, the image of her had been shaken from his mind.

He was distracted from these confused recollections by a raised voice outside, and he rose unsteadily and went to the shuttered window to look out.

The street was empty. A small dog crossed it from one side to the other. He felt faint at having risen so abruptly, and leaned against the wall for support.

He gathered up the papers of his unfinished report, but then let them fall to the floor as again his energies failed him.

Later, he heard from the girl who brought him water, and who sought only to leave the room before he spoke to her, that

141

the stonemason's daughter had gone missing. She had broken the clasp on a door and fled from her father during the night.

'Do they have any idea where she might have gone?' It was as much as he could ask; the village had been the world to her.

The girl shook her head. She was less anxious now that he had spoken to her, and it occurred to him that he might have earlier frightened her by calling out in his sleep while she was present in the room.

There was a further commotion in the street outside, this time the unmistakable clamour of the flock of geese which wandered freely around the village. The girl went to the window, but instead of looking down she gazed up into the sky and nodded at what she saw there.

'What is it?' he asked her.

'Wild fowl. They come over us every autumn on their way elsewhere.'

'And the creatures below – do they perhaps sense something of their own lost wildness?'

'I wouldn't know,' she said dismissively, and left him.

He waited until she had descended the stairs before going himself to the window and watching the rippling arrowhead skeins pass distantly overhead.

27

Samuel Mercer came the next day. The Inquisitor woke to see him sitting beside the fire. He pushed himself up and drew the bedsheets around him, but the magistrate did not turn to face him, and he saw that some part of the pact into which both of them had entered at their first meeting, though now impossibly fragile, remained unbroken.

Several minutes passed. The rules were to be observed.

The Inquisitor was the first to speak. 'Have they found the girl?'

Deception had become lie, and lie built upon lie, ever multiplying and spreading, like crystals of frost across a pane of glass.

The magistrate continued to stare into the flames. 'No.'

'Do you believe they will?'

It is said of a dying tree that for seven days before it is ready to fall it will shed a branch in warning to let those working near by be clear of it when the day of its crash arrives. Similarly, it is said that when an old dog becomes aware of its imminent death it will refuse to drink any water that is set down for it, or water that flows in a stream, and will drink instead only raindrops before they hit the ground. There are countless witnesses to their animals sitting out in storms with their mouths open to the clouds; there is nothing that can be done for them.

The magistrate shook his head, reconsidered, and then nodded.

As ever, the Inquisitor understood him perfectly, and both men retraced their steps back into the silence from which they might begin anew.

'You tipped the body back into its resting place,' Samuel Mercer said eventually.

'And the grave has been sealed?'

'By unwilling hands, but yes.'

'I've been sick, a fever. It need form no part of my report. No one wishes to know.'

Another man might have turned to him with an accusing finger and shouted 'Liar!'

'No one but you.'

'Is that why you came?'

The magistrate fell to silence for several minutes longer, harnessing the waters for his wave of revelation. This was how he himself thought of what he was doing, and the irony of it caused him to smile and eased open the first of his sluices.

'He was a drainer. The Dutchman.'

'Not a mercenary?'

'No. One of Vermuyden's men brought in by the King to attend to the draining of the Fens. He abandoned his work during the riots, driven out by the Tigers. How proud they must have felt, common labourers and watermen to have been called that.'

'I thought he'd been killed simply because he was an outsider, and a witness to what happened to the woman.'

'I cannot paint the picture any clearer for you. He and she formed a liaison. He found work with the old Lord Kepwick, draining his land. His countrymen, most of them unwilling to return home, were already at work in the neighbouring parishes.'

144

'But not this one. Is that why the land elsewhere, between here and the city, appears so fertile, while here everything remains—'

'As it always was? Yes. Drained land led to a doubling of rents, and then a doubling again the year after. You see what we are here, how we live. You must surely see what would have happened to us.'

The Inquisitor could not accept this, but remained silent. He understood more clearly the reasoning of his masters.

'Drain the land and fortunes are made in surplus only for those who own it. Men are gathered into bondage. Drain the land and roads come, outsiders arrive, holdings are taken from the poor and leased only to those men willing and able to increase their yields and turn their necessary profits. It was a time of terrible change and disruption.' Samuel Mercer shook his head.

'And you had seen it happening all around you, seen it coming closer and closer. You were never afraid of the Plague; it was this which made you fearful. Killing the woman was an excuse, done to disguise your motive for killing the man.'

'No! You must not believe that. Everything I told you about the woman was true.'

'But none of it helped by her relationship with this foreign devil.'

The magistrate looked up at the word. He could not deny it. 'We cannot all be raised and schooled in centres of commerce and free-thinking.'

'But you yourself – you surely must have seen the benefits to be gained by improving the land. You were not born here.'

'Of course I saw them.'

'Then why become a part of it all? Why, by your refusal to act on behalf of the man and the woman, endorse their persecution?'

145

'It was murder. I do not hide from the truth. We must all dwell within our own skins.'

'Then why?'

'I cannot tell you. I cannot plead ignorance in the matter, but I truly believe that an overall tide of events conspired against the couple.' He paused. 'Will you insist upon exhumation?'

The Inquisitor considered this and shook his head.

'No one lied to you about the woman. To the people here she was all the things they accused her of being. She became possessed by demons. She never denied her congress with them. She was seen during the nights with them. Despite what Jonas Webster might believe, there is sworn and written testimony to all this.'

'But not seen by you, surely?'

'No, not by me. I was victim enough of my own torments by then. My wife died in childbirth only days before the woman herself was killed. There is no redress to be made.'

'And you believe that the death of your wife was sufficient to tip the scales of reason and justice against her? Were you so intimately and irrevocably connected?'

The magistrate did not answer.

'Then tell me this – did Jonas Webster lead the persecuting mob? Did he have the most to lose to her and the man? Did he incite the others to their killing and destruction? Is that why he alone struggles so fervently now to make amends?' It was what the Inquisitor, in his dislike of the man, wanted to believe.

'I believe he never afterwards came to peace with himself. He had hoped one day to become bishop.'

'With blood on his hands?'

Both men regretted the remark.

'Condemn him and you condemn us all.'

But most of all, I condemn you, the Inquisitor thought.

'Were you at the killings, the burning and destruction?'

146

'No. My wife lay awaiting her removal by her parents. I sat with her without sleep for four days and four nights.'

'I apologize.'

'It seemed little enough penance at the time.'

'But you knew what was happening.'

The magistrate nodded. 'The day before the woman died she was brought to the church, fastened to a pillar, and her confession extracted.'

'By what means?'

'It matters not.'

'Then I must imagine.'

'Of course. But remember this, in imagining you do no more or less than the innocent, the blind, and the ignorant here who flocked to the church to hear for themselves what she had to say.'

'Then the village truly has seen an Inquisition. In which case, I relinquish the title, and hope never—'

'She was killed here,' the magistrate said unexpectedly. 'In the church and upon the hillside. She was taken outside so that her prince might rise up and rescue her. She was taken out so that he might be goaded into responding, that he might reveal himself and justify everything that had been done to her.'

'And he never came.'

'We know not. She was found dead in the morning.'

'So regardless of whether or not he came to her, you still considered your actions to be justified.'

'The Dutchman discovered what had happened and said he would ride to the city and return with the sheriff.'

'And thus condemned himself.'

'He was condemned already.'

'And killed when the house was destroyed.'

Samuel Mercer bowed his head. His reserve of energy was spent, and the revelation had been no release. Strong light

147

from the window fell in upon him and dissolved him in its glare. Motes of dust and ash rose around him.

By half closing his eyes, the Inquisitor could make him disappear completely; it was what the man wanted. Only the shadow of the hanging charm pierced this molten light and showed the magistrate's face, his trembling lips and unmoving eyes.

'Do you believe the missing girl has taken her own life, somewhere, perhaps, where she will never be found?' the Inquisitor said eventually, hoping to draw him from his trance and transport him from the past back to the present. But the old man did not answer him, did not even nod to let him know that he had heard the question.

28

He did not leave his room for a further two days.

He went first to the hill and saw there the completed angel, the great carved hands become doves in peaceful reward of benediction; white mouth close-lipped; flint eyes gazing coldly down on the souls he was risen to cleanse; forgiveness falling from every crease in his robe, flowing outlined in his cheeks and hair and swan-feather wings.

'Mocker,' whispered the Inquisitor, knowing that what had once been known only in the impenetrable hearts of men might now be seen and imperfectly understood by anyone with eyes to see and a mind to reason at abomination. He saw the abandoned woman dead at his feet.

He said a prayer where he stood, as though by this means alone he might wipe the figure from his own eyes and mind. But he knew he was wrong to expect so much, and knew too that his dreams and visions would be for ever afterwards invaded. And he knew that because of this his dreams would soon cease, and with them his passion for the work to which he devoted himself.

Everything he now saw and heard in this place fell upon him like a rock and crushed some new bone in his body.

Earlier, he had enquired about leaving and was told that a horse might be brought for him in three days. The same knowing and uncommunicative man who had brought him would gather him up and take him away. He had asked about the coach bringing the magistrate's son the following morning, but was told that its hirers would countenance no other use of it, and that it would return to them empty, then be sent back empty a week later to pick up its sole passenger. For the magistrate's sake, he did not contest this wastefulness, and was anyway content to be taken away as he had been delivered, crowned with suspicion and resentment, and making easy his severance of the place once he was out of sight of it.

Vapours rose from the river and stirred the stubble smoke which still hung above the blackened fields. Smaller fires burned untended for days, like candles of devotion or powders of incense in a temple. Here and there a man or woman still worked in the fields, and they passed him in the village without speaking, their faces lowered or turned away from him. A word from his lips and they might turn instantly to the ash of their guilt or the salt of their remorse.

He waited inside the churchyard until Jonas Webster was drawn out to speak to him. And with him came his wife, her cheeks wet with tears.

'You see our work is completed,' Jonas Webster said, indicating the angel. Only his wife turned to look up at the great figure floating above them.

'And all your sins washed clean?'

'The Lord forgives us.'

'And you, Mistress Webster, does the Lord forgive you, too?'

The crying woman looked from the Inquisitor to her husband, waiting for her answer from his lips. She was not the woman who had visited the Inquisitor in his room, merely an empty shell drained of her husband's once sustaining longings and preparations.

'Just as He forgives us, so the Lord understands us. It is

His work we undertake here, His work in which we seek our reward.'

'And His platitudes which become hurdles drawn around you at the onset of night, and each longer darker night drawn a little closer.'

The woman started to weep more openly and loudly, and held her hands to her face until her tears pooled in her palms and then ran down the backs of her fingers.

The Inquisitor pointed to the church. 'I wonder that the place hasn't ever afterwards been filled with screams.'

'Perhaps it has,' Jonas Webster said scornfully. 'Perhaps it has, and perhaps everyone here hears them.' He grabbed his wife by the arm and shook her. Then, pulling her alongside him, he walked her back into their home. She stumbled as she went, but he showed her no compassion.

The Inquisitor waited in the silence of their departure, hearing only the childlike cries of curlews high above the moor. He saw that by his actions and his demands a powerful vacuum had been created, and one into which anything might now be drawn.

From the church he went to the stonemason's yard. He found it empty. He searched the buildings, but the man was not there. On his way back out he almost fell over a piece of stone, and looking down he saw that what had tripped him was a carved head. And realizing this he looked slowly around him at his audience of decapitated bodies, and each one wrested a sigh or an inward groan of disbelief from him. Faces took shape amid the boulders and debris at his feet, and he stared at them almost in a state of shock, as any man might look at them who had wandered so unknowingly into that place of execution.

29

Later in the day, feeling the need for fresher air to clear his head, he passed unnoticed through the houses and walked on the moor. He followed paths and walked on ground that was recently burned. He regretted that he had not been able to discover the location of the woman's grave, but it was not his purpose now, and he knew that even if Samuel Mercer had volunteered to direct him to it he would still not have been wholly convinced of what he was being shown.

He walked south, a direction he had never before taken, and wished he could have reached the edge of that barren upland and looked down over the fertile plain below.

After walking for two hours he sat to rest, and when he rose he saw a party of women working close by. He was about to approach and greet them when he saw that he did not recognize them. They were not from the village, but from some other. Their clothes were more colourful, their conversation punctuated by laughter, and their hair was long and blonde. He had wandered further than he realized, and he instinctively crouched down so as not to alarm them by his sudden appearance in so isolated a place. Their laughter grew briefly louder and then faded, and he waited until he could scarcely hear them before rising and watching them walk away from him. He watched them until they disappeared, envious of their uninhibited amusement and carefree familiarity.

He had come as far as he dare go and so he turned back. In another age he might have chosen the life of a hermit and wandered ceaselessly. The notion amused him, and perhaps because his spirits had been raised by the laughter of the women he himself laughed aloud.

He returned to familiar surroundings.

Another party of women crossed his path, and this time he recognized them immediately. They saw him but did not call out to him or wait for him to reach them. Instead they all turned and considered him for a moment and then resumed their journey home, making it clear to him that they did not wish him to join them. It was another tie severed, and though of less consequence than those already lost he felt it keenly. His first impulse had been to run and catch up with them, but he waited where he stood until they too were out of sight.

They are all in mourning for themselves, he thought. The whole village was.

He paused again at the edge of the moor and looked down at the houses, now more clearly revealed to him through the leafless branches. Smoke rose slowly in the cold air, gathered, and hung in a pall.

As he contemplated this, he heard voices behind him, and turning he saw in the distance Jonas Webster and his two veterans. They had not seen him, and he moved away from the path and settled himself in a hollow so he might watch and overhear them unobserved.

The three men came on slowly, pausing frequently to rest. Most of the conversation was between the two labourers. Jonas Webster walked several paces ahead of them, a Bible held to his chest. Stump and Jaw carried sledgehammers, and each time they paused they let these fall to the ground.

The Inquisitor rose at their approach. Jonas Webster was the first to see him, and he immediately silenced the others.

'We thought you was gone,' Jaw said.

Stump prodded Jonas Webster. 'You said he was gone.'

Jonas Webster only smiled. He raised the Bible until it rested beneath his chin. 'Gone soon enough,' he said. 'Gone soon enough.' His eyes never left the Inquisitor's.

'What's he doing up here?'

'Spying on us.'

'I believe his spying is over,' Jonas Webster said. 'Whatever happens now is of no consequence to him.' His smile hardened. 'Am I correct in my assumption, Inquisitor?'

The Inquisitor said nothing.

Behind Jonas Webster, Jaw raised his hammer and let it drop.

'We have had a long hard day, my friends and I,' Jonas Webster said.

'A ten-mile round trip.'

'And him with only the one good leg.'

Both men laughed at this.

The Inquisitor knew immediately where they had been and the purpose of their visit.

Jonas Webster saw this and nodded in confirmation.

'Destroyed,' he said. 'I doubt if even you could find it now, Inquisitor. Work we should have finished a decade ago.'

'When we smashed off the top.' Stump swung his hammer into the path.

'Stones now,' Jonas Webster said. 'Scattered in all directions.' He came forward and the others followed him. He kissed the Bible and held it high above him as though it were a flaming torch to light their way through the falling dusk.

The Inquisitor stood aside and watched them go, and when they had gone he looked back in the direction they had come. But that quarter of the world was already plunged into darkness, and the path at his feet turned grey and then black as

154

it drew away from him, looking more and more like a fast-flowing river the further it receded, ceaseless, urgent and unbending, and more certain than any man who ever followed it of its destination and its drop at the edge of the world.

30

He sat alone and read again the few unrewarding pages of his report, and afterwards he composed his equally unsatisfactory letter of resignation. He did this now because here, this place, was where he had made the decision, and because he knew that upon leaving it his resolve would weaken.

It was the eve of his departure and the empty hours of waiting stretched ahead of him. All he knew of the following day was that the carter would arrive to collect him some time between noon and dusk.

Samuel Mercer's son had arrived the previous day and he planned to visit the man that evening.

The village was empty. A first frost had been predicted, and the water in the rutted street looked ready to turn to ice.

He went directly to the magistrate's house and knocked on the door. No one answered. He knocked again, but still received no reply. He stood back, looked up, and saw that smoke rose from the chimney. A sound deep inside the house drew him back to the door, but still no one came. There were other sounds – the sound of wood struck against wood and the sound of something, crockery perhaps, being cleared or dropped.

Intrigued, he left the front of the house and followed the narrow path along the side of the building. Light fell from a rear window, and he recognized this as the room in which he and the magistrate had always met, the room in which the man had always sought to deny the passage of time, and the only place, it now occurred to the Inquisitor, where he had ever felt completely secure and beyond all sight and reproach of the world. He hesitated, uncertain whether to announce himself at the window, knock at the rear door, or return to the front and knock more loudly there. But before he could decide, an outline crossed the lighted square and a shadow fell at his feet. He could not see to whom this belonged, and he stepped out of reach of it as it slid across the ground towards him.

Certain that he had not been seen, he returned to the window. He looked inside, and nothing he had so far seen or heard or imagined prepared him for what he saw there.

For there was the magistrate sitting by the fire, and in his arms, naked except for the soiled cloth fastened around his waist, was a man more skin and bone than muscle and flesh, a man who had no control over his limbs, and whose skin was white and smeared and dotted with bruises; whose neck was long and arched and whose overlarge head rested on its side upon one shoulder; whose eyes moved uncontrollably back and forth, and who slavered copiously down his chin and chest; whose spine was curved, whose arms were twisted at unnatural angles, whose bony hands were folded in on themselves, and whose elbows were raised and looked more like the wings of a plucked chicken than human limbs; whose large dirty feet rested on the floor but supported no weight, and whose knees were swollen, discoloured and bleeding. And all this wretchedness, this deformity, this joke and mockery of a man lay folded in the magistrate's arms.

The Inquisitor stood transfixed, barely breathing, and barely able to comprehend all that he saw. He moved closer

157

until he could see more widely into the room. The man and the man-child were alone, illuminated only by the dull glow of the fire and the flicker of the candles out of reach on the table.

The magistrate caressed his son's head, his hair slubbed black and brown and grey, and made soothing sounds close to his ear. He rocked him gently and suppressed his every movement. The child responded by flapping his folded arms and rolling his head. He opened his twisted mouth in delight, but could only grunt and then let fall another long stream of saliva. The magistrate spoke to him, stroking his cheek, and again the boy flapped his arms in response.

The Inquisitor stepped away from the window.

Here was the malformed child that had been born and lived while its mother died.

Here, at last, was the pole of radiating connections joining every line of longitude which girdled that violated place. And here, above all else, were the entwined serpents of threat and promise that had for so long and so firmly sealed the pact between Samuel Mercer and Jonas Webster and everyone else within the same small self-regarding orbit around them.

The Inquisitor stepped further back. A branch snapped at his feet and he froze at the centre of the light which fell from the window.

He looked back inside. The magistrate was staring directly at him, his face still pressed to his son's wet cheek, his hand still caressing his head. Then he grasped the boy's face, raised it from where it rested on his shoulder and turned it to face the window. It was not done in warning or anger, not meant to threaten or to silence, but done because now that the terrible secret was shared, there was no other way to acknowledge the fact.

Again the Inquisitor stood transfixed. The eyes of the

child did not look back at him, but instead rolled from side to side in confusion, one wide open, the other half closed; his tongue lolled loosely over his wet lips.

Then the magistrate lowered his son's head back to his chest, and, waiting until the child was calmed, he turned to the Inquisitor and mouthed the word *wait*.

Before the Inquisitor could respond, the door into the room opened and the housekeeper entered with a bowl of water and a cloth. She stopped when she saw the magistrate and then she too turned to face the Inquisitor.

He looked away from her and saw the broken crockery and spilled food which covered the floor at her feet.

When he looked back she was already lifting the skeletal figure from the magistrate's lap.

Relieved of his burden, Samuel Mercer rose, came to the window and indicated the rear door.

He emerged a moment later. Saliva glistened on his jacket and shirt, and he dabbed at this with his handkerchief.

'My son,' he said, warm breath wreathing his face. There was neither shame nor remorse in his voice, and he held up his hand so that the Inquisitor would not interrupt him. 'It had always been my intention to name him Christopher after the protector saint of travellers and guardian of the mermaids.' There was affection and distant longing in his voice. 'But instead, when, in less than a minute, my beloved wife was dead and he was born and I knew that he would be taken from me, I named him Matthew. From the gospel.'

'Don't,' the Inquisitor said.

But the magistrate went on. '"Lord have mercy on my son for he is lunatic and sore vexed, for oft-times he falleth into the fire, and oft into the water."' He spoke now in a trance of contentment.

159

The Inquisitor completed the reading. '"And Jesus rebuked the devil in the child and he departed out of him, and the child was cured from that very hour."'

'Alas not.' Samuel Mercer held his hands to his face.

'It is my name also,' the Inquisitor said, bewildered, disbelieving, as though so long unused it was something he had momentarily forgotten. It was beyond him to reach out and hold the man, to comfort him as he had held and comforted his son, and after several minutes of silence, he backed slowly away from him, out of the pool of light in which they stood, and out of reach of any hand that might suddenly seize him and draw him back. And only when he was completely immersed in darkness did he turn and run.

He ran until his heart grew wild in his chest, and until sweat flowed from his brow and dripped from his chin. He ran past the houses and along the road leading to the Vale, not knowing if he intended returning for his few belongings, or if he would run until daybreak, until noon, until dark, until he met the man sent to fetch him, or until he met the road home and could follow it secure in the knowledge of where it led.

He ran distracted, buried deep in his thoughts and useless speculations, and when for the first time he stopped and looked up, alerted by some strange sound ahead of him, he saw coming towards him through the darkness the hushed white hands of an owl, aimed directly at him, opening and closing, beseeching and beckoning, and he shielded his face and cried out, and the bird, itself so suddenly disturbed, faltered in its flight, veered to one side, and was immediately lost to him within its own impenetrable domain of night.